DEADLY THINGS

A COLLECTION OF MYSTERIOUS TALES

DARRELL SCHWEITZER

[signed] Darrell Schweitzer
Boskone 2011

THE BORGO PRESS
MMXI

DEADLY THINGS

Copyright © 1990, 1994, 1996, 1997, 1998, 2003,
2007, 2008, 2011 by Darrell Schweitzer
[p. 9-10 shall serve as an extension to this copyright page]

FIRST EDITION

Published by Wildside Press LLC

www.wildsidebooks.com

DEDICATION

For Beverly Potter,

Who might appreciate this
more than my usual effusions

CONTENTS

Acknowledgments 9

Some Unpublished Correspondence of the Younger Pliny . . 11

The Stolen Venus 31

Last Things 51

In a Byzantine Garden 67

The Death of Falstaff 71

Murdered by Love 85

The Adventure of the Death-Fetch 103

Sherlock Holmes, Dragon-Slayer 125

The Adventure of the Hanoverian Vampires 141

About the Author 149

ACKNOWLEDGMENTS

THESE STORIES WERE previously published as follows, and are reprinted (with some editing, updating, and textual modifications) by permission of the author:

"Some Unpublished Correspondence of the Younger Pliny" was first published in *The Mammoth Book of Roman Whodunnits* edited by Mike Ashley. Copyright © 2003, 2011 by Darrell Schweitzer.

"The Stolen Venus" was first published in *Alfred Hitchcock's Mystery Magazine* October 2008. Copyright © 2008, 2011 by Dell Magazines.

"Last Things" was first published in *The Mammoth Book of Classical Whodunits* edited by Mike Ashley. Copyright © 1996, 2011 by Darrell Schweitzer.

"In a Byzantine Garden" was first published in *Paradox* #11, Autumn 2007. Copyright © 2007 by Paradox; Copyright © 2011 by Darrell Schweitzer.

"The Death of Falstaff" was first published in *Shakespearean Whodunnits* edited by Mike Ashley. Copyright © 1997, 2011 by Darrell Schweitzer.

"Murdered by Love" was published in *Shakespearean Detectives* edited by Mike Ashley. Copyright © 1998, 2011 by Darrell Schweitzer.

"The Adventure of the Death-Fetch" was first published in *The Game Is Afoot* edited by Marvin Kaye. Copyright © 1994, 2011 by Darrell Schweitzer.

"Sherlock Holmes, Dragon-Slayer" was first published in

Resurrected Holmes edited by Marvin Kaye. Copyright © 1996 by Darrell Schweitzer.

"The Adventure of the Hanoverian Vampires" was first published in *100 Crafty Cat Crimes*, edited by Martin Greenberg, Stefan Dziemianowicz, and Robert Weinberg. Barnes & Noble Books, 1990. Copyright © 1990, 2011 by Darrell Schweitzer.

SOME UNPUBLISHED CORRESPONDENCE OF THE YOUNGER PLINY

1. *Pliny to the Emperor Trajan*

I have written to you previously, Sir, about my encounter in Bithynia with persons vulgarly called "Christians," and have gratefully received your advice on how such criminals are to be dealt with, which ones are to be spared, and which offered up to punishment.

I discovered, in the course of my investigations, as I have previously mentioned, that these persons comprise a degenerate cult carried to ridiculous lengths, but that through the moderating influence of the law, many persons might be reformed and directed back to the correct worship of our gods.

The affair has, however, had a kind of sequel. If I may trouble you again with a long description of these matters, I would like to describe the case of a young girl, which seems to press beyond the bounds of the practical guidelines you have given me. If I were a the right kind of poet I would find here the material for a tragedy, dealing as it does with the themes of young lovers and love lost, of conflict between a father and his child, the delicate balance between justice and compassion, and the mysteries of the world of the dead.

I shall not waste your time with fancies, however. You, who bear on your shoulders the responsibility for nothing less than the welfare of all mankind, will doubtless want to know only the facts....

2. *Trajan to Pliny.*

 Before you departed on your mission, my dear Pliny, I took you aside and requested that you write to me whenever you felt the impulse to do so, not merely in an official capacity dealing with finances and waterworks, but as a friend might to another friend, to share the experience of his journey with another who is far away and cannot see and hear what he himself sees and hears.

3. *Pliny to Trajan.*

 ...I proceeded from Nicomedia to the shore of the Euxine Sea, and there my party followed the road through one town after the other, staying at the homes of prominent citizens, dealing with such matters as might need to be dealt with. I am accompanied, as you know, by two very capable men, both of whom you met at least briefly before I departed from Rome. They are my Greek physician, a freedman called Arpocras, a wise and inquisitive fellow, whom I fondly call, when he is not within hearing, Little Aristotle, for, like that philosopher he inquires into all things tirelessly; and, secondly, my assistant Servilius Pudens, a Roman knight of unquestionable reliability and loyalty. This Pudens is, however, of a more choleric disposition, easily excited, and quick to leap to conclusions, but sensible enough (especially when moderated by Arpocras's cooler judgments) not to *act* upon his conclusions until he is more certain of them. I call the pair—when both are out of earshot—my two crows, for their frequent arguments may sound like strident squawking, but in fact they share a kind of philosophical discourse.
 It happened on that afternoon when we arrived at Heracleia Pontica, as these two (who shared the carriage with me) were in

the middle of some furious sparring-match about which of the heroes of the Trojan War had journeyed through these regions in ages past, and whether or not the local monuments to this or that legendary person were of merit or merely a means for the locals to beguile a few coppers out of the gullible traveler... as this well-chewed-over argument drifted somewhere between comedy and tedium, sufficient to distract me for the moment from the documents I was glancing through...at this juncture a runner from the town approached and announced that he was a servant of one L. Catius Magnus, who most earnestly desired that we dine with him that night.

"Well, I shall be glad to be free of the dust of the road, and other discomforts," said Arpocras, rolling his eyes toward Servilius Pudens.

"I? I am classified as a discomfort? I am a hardship of the journey?" said Pudens, mortified, as if he were about to leap out of the carriage and stalk all the way back to Rome, which is an absurdity, because the over-large, ever-sweating Pudens would hardly have lasted a mile in the heat. But this was for show, as always. Their friendship is never threatened by such displays.

"We could afford to relax and spend a pleasant evening," I said.

Arpocras's gaunt—indeed, crow-like—features narrowed, and he spoke in a low voice. "I think there is more than relaxation here. This Catius Magnus seems a trifle over-eager to make our acquaintance."

"It's obvious enough," said Pudens. "He wants to be seen entertaining the Emperor's own representative, to make himself seem more important. It's a great way to impress the natives."

"I don't deny that, friend Pudens. Nevertheless, I think there is more to it than that."

"Indeed, we shall see," I said, in the tone of a judge, hoping to make peace between them, for, indeed, I was weary from the journey, my head had begun to ache, and just now I was not in a humor to be amused by two squawking crows.

It turned out that Lucius Catius Magnus offered us every

possible comfort. He stood at the doorway of his house as our company approached. Indeed, we must have looked to the locals like an invading army, possibly a hundred persons in all, myself, my staff, servants, many carriages and wagons, and a troop of mounted guards bringing up the rear. All were accommodated. The soldiers and most of the servants camped in a vacant space nearby. Catius Magnus, perceptively discerning that Arpocras and Pudens were more than mere functionaries, invited the three of us to bathe and dine with him.

So the hours passed pleasantly enough. After bathing, we strolled in the cool evening breeze beneath a colonnade, at the edge of a vineyard. The scenery was extremely attractive. I could almost imagine myself back in Italy, gazing out, not over the Euxine, but the Bay of Neapolis toward Capreae. This Magnus had made every effort to transplant a bit of home, here in Bithynia, or, perhaps I should put it, to make at least a patch of this foreign soil truly Roman.

Magnus himself turned out to be a man somewhat younger than myself, about thirty-five, the twice-great grandson of a soldier who had served with Pompey and helped colonize the area when he retired. The family had prospered through investments and trade. By the standards, at least, of a provincial town, they had grown great. Magnus, like his father and grandfather before him, was a member of the local senate. His family held several priesthoods. He himself officiated over regular sacrifices to the gods, to the Emperor's genius, and also to the spirit of the Divine Augustus, whose small temple the local senators maintained at their own expense.

Magnus went on in this vein—gods, sacrifices, rites, loyalty—for more than I thought ordinary. It piqued my curiosity. Indeed, when, over dinner, I exchanged a glance with my ever-alert Arpocras, he seemed to reply wordlessly, *Ah, we near the heart of the matter.*

Pudens winked. When he is impatient, one side of his face twitches in an odd way.

So we came to the heart of it, suddenly. Imagine some mishap in the theater and an actor's mask suddenly falls off. There is his face, revealed, dismayed, and he has no secrets anymore.

Catius Magnus interrupted his own small-talk.

"Sir," he burst out, "the reason I've brought you here, what I'm really after...is mercy...mercy for my only child, my beloved daughter Catia...."

"What?" exclaimed Pudens, who sounded as if he'd nearly choked.

Arpocras and I exchanged knowing glances.

I bade Catius Magnus explain, trying to be reassuring in my manner. He was almost unmanned by whatever troubled him, close to tears.

Explain he did, somewhat incoherently, though this was, of course, an educated and articulate man. Yes, he had a daughter. I had seen her briefly when we entered the house, a pretty girl of fourteen or fifteen, who had bowed to me demurely, then been led away with apparent haste by two large serving-women. At the time I had wondered if the girl might be ill. Now it was clear.

The girl was, or professed to be, despite her father's every effort to dissuade her, one of "those of Christ," called "Chrestianoi" by the vulgar provincials. She had been led into this vice by a servant—who had since been disposed of—a lewd woman who acted as pander between the headstrong Catia and her lover, one Charicles, son of Damon. Now Catius Magnus knew Damon slightly through his business, a respectable enough fellow, a grain merchant, pious enough in his observances of the gods. Prejudice aside, the match might not have been impossible. True, Damon and his son were not even Roman citizens, but Greeks—and when this was mentioned, my good Arpocras shot me an offended glance, as if to say, *And what is wrong with that?*

Otherwise young Charicles was handsome and pleasant, and his family was rich. Not impossible, though he could be nearly as wild as the girl.

So Charicles and Catia became lovers in secret, and in secret descended into much more serious matters. They became

Christians. Using various deceits, with the full connivance of Catia's servant, they secreted themselves, night after night, to a necropolis outside the city, where they participated in the abominable rites of the *Chrestianoi*. The leader of the cult seemed to be some awesome personage, a thaumaturge called the Masked One, who promised, among other things, that his followers would live forever in the flesh and need never fear death. This presumably would allow them to continue in carnal rites until the end of time, when their dead Christ would also rise from the dead, return to them, cast down the gods and rule the world.

"Of course...of course...." Catius Magnus was almost too beside himself to continue speaking. "It is *complete rubbish*. I knew it. Damon knew it—"

"Damon knew it?" Arpocras asked.

"Yes, yes. He did. *As one father to another,* he came to me. He asked *my* help. He was as appalled as I...."

"I should think," interrupted Pudens, "that a father would be able to control his daughter, and another—even if he is a Greek—"

Arpocras cleared his throat irritably. Pudens continued.

"—even if he is a Greek would be able to control his son."

"Have you any children, Sir?" Catius said with surprising sharpness. It put Pudens off his balance.

"No, I don't."

I waved my hand dismissively, and Pudens said nothing more. To Catius Magnus I said, "Nor do I. Friend Arpocras has two sons, who are far away. But I think we understand—"

"Can you, Sir? Can you really? Can you appreciate how a father's love for his child might come into conflict with his duty?"

"Duty must prevail," I said quietly.

"Indeed, Sir, it must. Damon and I resolved to do our duty. I ordered my daughter kept under close watch. I got rid of the evil serving-woman. Damon was going to send his son away on a *very* long trading trip away north somewhere—across the sea, wherever they get amber. It seemed like a good idea at the time.

But then your instructions were published—"

"I was but repeating those of the Emperor himself, who graciously advised me," I said.

"Of course. Caesar's guidelines cannot be questioned. And, I assure you, none of the local officials did question them. That was Damon's grief. It broke his heart. It killed him well before his time."

"Killed him?" Arpocras asked, "How?"

I could sense the man's true grief, his own fear, his confusion, his desire to fulfill his duty as a Roman citizen, and I he had only my deepest sympathy. Here was a man who would do, I was sure, the brave and correct thing at the end.

"It killed him, by the failure of his heart, when the police began to inquire after Christians, and, far from attempting to hide his guilt, the young fool Charicles proclaimed his allegiance openly. He even named Catia as a fellow conspirator. He laughed at the judges, claiming that he had no fear of them at all, because death could not touch him, that if they killed him, he would be resurrected immediately. Now, shocking as all of this was, we couldn't quite put it out of our minds that this was one of our neighbors, a child had played in our streets, who might yet be saved if properly guided. Damon wept and got down on his knees, begging his son to repent. Others enjoined him. I did. But in the end I had to try to save my daughter. She shrieked like a fury when brought into the court, clawing at the women who restrained her. That, I think, inadvertently helped, because I was able to convince the judges that she was mad. In the end, though, Charicles was crucified, and Damon, with a dignity that would befit even a Roman, merely announced that he would retire to his house and not emerge again. He died within a few days."

There was a long pause. Night had long since fallen. Within the house, we were shielded from both city noises and those of nature. Silence prevailed, in the gathering dark. A servant entered the room, offering to refill everyone's wine cups, but was waved away.

Pudens, large and corpulent fellow as he is, squirmed uneasily as he reclined. The couch creaked.

"A truly terrible story," I said at last, "but I don't see how I can actually help you. The girl is under no legal judgment, having been declared insane. Perhaps Arpocras, who is very learned in the medicines of the Greeks, can prepare a potion to calm her mind."

"Thank you," said Catius Magnus. "Thank you...." For a moment he seemed too emotionally exhausted to say much more. But then he rallied. "I fear...what I am truly afraid of...is that this matter is *not over.* Nothing is over with. The Masked One of the *Chrestianoi* still haunts the night. Some of his followers have been caught, but they will not give up his secret. My daughter would tell nothing, even—"

"There are ways, you know," Pudens said, "to get anybody to confess anything."

"Gods!" exclaimed Arpocras. With one savage look he shut up Pudens. I could only concur. We were hardly going to ask Catius Magnus to torture his own daughter!

It took some persuading to get him to continue, but at last I got the extraordinary heart of the story out of him.

"The matter is not over," he said, "not merely because some masked criminal is still on the loose, *but because his promises have turned out to be true. His followers can indeed transcend death. I know this is so. The boy Charicles has come back from the dead and I myself have seen him!"*

Now *that,* I confess, put even me at a loss. I believe there are such things as ghosts. I had a long discussion with Licinius Sura on the matter once. Both of us knew many stories. The one about the philosopher Athenodorus renting the haunted house, wherein he discovered and laid to rest a chained spirit, is rather famous. But *what,* I could only ask myself, was I, as an Imperial representative charged with legal and financial investigations, supposed to do? I wasn't sure I had any jurisdiction over ghosts.

It was Arpocras who came to my rescue, who cut his way through the dark clouds of superstition which were gathered all about us.

"What, exactly, did you see, Sir?"

"First I *heard.* The servants told me that the girl was talking to someone in the night, calling out in the darkness. The servants were terrified. They thought she was summoning demons. I thought, alas, that she really was mad, and it wasn't just a convenient plea to save her life for a time. But to be sure I stood by the door to her chamber one night—and I heard her call out, addressing her beloved Charicles—and, incredible though this may seem, I heard the boy reply. I recognized the voice. It *was* Charicles."

"But you didn't see him?"

"Oh, I saw. He said he would return again when the Moon was dark. I don't know what that means. Perhaps the *Chrestianoi* fear the Moon Goddess. Anyway, I said nothing to my daughter, but noted how as the time of the dark of the Moon approached, she grew calmer, but more anxious, as if *expectant.* This time I did what might sound a little ridiculous. I climbed up on the roof of our house. There I was above my daughter's room. Her window looks out over the sheds and stables by our wall, into the street, where there is a broad space at the edge of a few trees, with a stone bench. You've seen the place.

"On the appointed night, then, with all the servants in their rooms at my orders, I watched from the roof. My daughter came to the window right below me. She called out something I couldn't quite make out, some kind of prayer or incantation, and *Charicles* answered. Her words then were of joy, of how much she loved him and wanted to be with him. He promised that she would be soon, despite anything her 'cruel jailer'—meaning me—could possibly do about it, because the power of the Masked One was greater than that of the whole Empire or even the gods. 'How can I know this?' says she. 'Please, give me some proof?' 'Isn't your faith strong enough, even after all we've been through?' 'I am afraid,' says she. 'I am weak. Please.' She wept piteously, and Charicles assented. *'Look at me, Catia. Do you not recognize me.'* There was a light over among those trees, as if someone had uncovered a lantern, and there *sitting on the bench* was the youth Charicles. He looked—though of course it was hard to tell under the circumstances—pale and *strange* in a way I could not quite define. But it was Charicles, all right. He raised his hand.

"At that point Catia let out a cry, and I was so startled, I admit, that I nearly lost my grip on the roof. I slipped. A couple of loose tiles crashed into the paved yard below, and the light among the trees went out. By the time I could clamber down and summon a couple of manservants, and we could get outside to those trees, we found only the empty bench. There was no sign that anyone had been there."

"No sign?" said Arpocras.

"What would you expect? We didn't find the lantern."

"How was your daughter?" I asked.

"The nurse found her on the floor. She had fallen into a swoon, which became a delirium, from which she has only imperfectly recovered."

"How long ago was this?"

"But two nights before you arrived in the city."

Again I wondered how I, who am trained as a lawyer and to some extent as an engineer, could be of any particular assistance. It continued to seem more a matter for a physician—or a priest.

Catius Magnus looked at me, helplessly.

"Couldn't you...make up some document...declaring her to be innocent because of her illness, now and into the future?"

I explained that no law can absolve someone for a crime they may commit in the future.

"Then I have no hope," said Catius Magnus. "It may take years, but this will destroy my daughter. As long as she thinks her boy is alive—as long as he *is alive*—she will believe in the magic of the *Chrestianoi*. I can only restrain her for so long. When she grows up, as an adult woman...perhaps after I am gone...she will continue to proclaim her adherence to these cultists. And she will have to be punished, as the Emperor's guidelines have clearly laid down. She will not recant, I am certain of that. So what am I to do? I can only pray uselessly to the gods, and mourn."

Again there was a moment of awkward silence, and again it was my indispensable Arpocras who saved us.

"I think we can help, Sir. I think we can look into this."

I saw that for once he and Pudens were of one mind. I didn't let on that I was the one who didn't quite follow.

****

...so we remained for several days as the guests of Catius Magnus. His daughter was kept out of sight. I inquired once of the serving women, and they said that "The Mistress" was sleeping calmly. There was no other mistress in this house, as Magnus's wife had died some years before and he had not remarried.

But she couldn't sleep all the time, could she, even if drugged? Sooner or later she would get into more trouble. I appreciated my host's dilemma.

Nevertheless, I kept myself occupied with official business. The financial records of Heraclia Pontica were in arrears, like those of so many others in this province. There were the usual improprieties, an aqueduct that cost three times as much as it should, a theatre that never seemed to be finished....

It was Arpocras who made more intimate inquiries. He asked to see the girl, and said that he found her awake, not at all delirious, but closely guarded by muscular women the size of small oxen, and the look on her face was one of absolute, venomous hatred for him and for all of us.

He went out into the town and asked certain questions.

One afternoon he deposited a small lump of matter on my desk.

"What is that?"

"Wax, Sir."

"So it is. What of it?"

"I found it on the bench across the street, by the trees."

"I confess I don't see the significance."

"If someone used the kind of lantern which has a candle in it, as opposed to an oil-lamp, it might leave such droppings."

"So? I am sure many of the citizens possess such lanterns."

"But I do not think they use them while sitting on that bench in the middle of the night."

"Perhaps that is so—"

"It means that someone was actually there, Sir, as Catius Magnus reported."

"I didn't think he was lying. You don't mean—?"

"No, Sir, I don't," he said, at his most inscrutable.

* * * * * * *

What we finally decided to do, following a suggestion which came, inevitably, from Arpocras, and to which I assented, was to actually attend one of the midnight orgies of the *Chrestianoi*. This was the only way to gain the answers we needed, and to bring our host's agony to an end.

It raised a tactical problem. It hadn't been too hard for Arpocras to learn when and roughly where the cultists met. It was an open secret among the lower orders of the town. Some dreaded these meetings as the manifestations of demons, which would bring plague and doom on us all. Others anticipated them. It seemed that the infection was quite widespread…and all too many believed the impossible, apocalyptic—a term the *Chrestianoi* used—prophecies of the Masked One. I had to admit that these were not at all like the beliefs of the criminals over whose trials I had presided at Nicomedia, but what respectable Roman can possibly know much about these strange matters? Is it possible that there are differing factions and even various nations of *Chrestianoi* right before our eyes, invisible to all but fellow believers?

But I drift from my theme. The immediate problem was how to attend the meeting without giving alarm. We tried, one last time, to convince the girl to cooperate.

She spat in Arpocras's face.

"You can kill me," she said, "but I will not betray them. I am not afraid of you."

Arpocras, showing a manner I had never before seen in him, yanked the girl's head back by the hair, held a small knife to her throat, and said, "We'll see how fearless you really are."

"Go ahead. I will rise again...as Charicles has risen and *you never will.*"

"It's useless, Arpocras," I said.

He let her go and put his knife away. He sighed. "Yes, it is. But I have something here which is not." He revealed a small, stoppered phial, which he set on a tabletop.

The two muscular serving-women held the girl Catia firmly while Arpocras forced her mouth open.

"Would you open that for me, please?" he said to Pudens, indicating the phial. Pudens opened it, and, as the Greek nodded, poured the contents down the girl's throat. He held his hand over her nose and mouth, and, struggle though she might, she eventually swallowed.

Her father looked away.

"She is not harmed," said Arpocras. "The potion will merely make her docile. She is unlikely to speak, but if she did, her words would be slurred, as if she were drunk. But if we guide her, she will be able to walk, and if we arrive in her company, and are not ourselves recognized, perhaps it will be enough." He looked at me, as if to say wordlessly, *It's the best I could come up with.*

It would have to do. All there was left for us to do was to disguise ourselves. Arpocras wore a Greek cloak. Catius Magnus, Pudens, and I wore the plain togas, of citizens, but without the stripes of a senator or a knight, which might attract too much attention. That the clothing we donned was not entirely clean was for the best.

We draped our togas up over our heads, like hoods, to hide our faces. We could only hope that perhaps the *Chrestianoi* maintained this custom of covering the head when at religious services...in any case, luck was with us. It looked like it was going to rain. It was a dark, windy, overcast night.

...And at the time appointed then, we made our way, the girl between us with her either arm held by Pudens and her father, out of the city of the living, into the city of the dead. There among the many tombs—some of them alleged to be of Homeric heroes; I could imagine Arpocras and Pudens chattering about them under happier circumstances—we waited, seated on a flat stone. We had with us a lantern with a candle inside it, but kept it covered.

I felt a little spray of rain on my face. The night was, indeed, turning foul. A storm approached from across the sea. The air started to turn cold. I saw that the girl Catia's teeth were chattering, even though the expression on her face was completely blank. She stared forward, into nothing.

But it was by following her gaze that I saw the first sign. A cloaked, furtive shape moved among the tombs. Then there was another, and another. They were all around us. I fancied for a second that we had been overwhelmed and surrounded by some army of beasts, something that crawled up out of the earth or out of graves.

Someone whistled. Someone else began to play, very faintly, on a flute.

"We cannot conceal ourselves," whispered Arpocras.

We stood up, Catius Magnus and Pudens holding the girl, Arpocras holding the covered lantern under his cloak.

There were little outcries of surprise, but then the cultists—for so they were, ordinary men and women and even a few children, all of the meaner sort—saw that the girl was with us, and this soothed them.

They parted before us and bade us proceed, and so we did proceed into a low area, where running water had cut away part of a hillside, and some of the tombs seemed about ready to tumble down on our heads. Far away, lightning flashed. Thunder came a while after. The rain was more than spray now, light, but persistent. I will admit that I was afraid, that every superstitious fear which we try to banish away by philosophy and reason came washing back over me like a tide. I feared the wrath of Hecate, absurd as that seemed. I feared hungry, angry ghosts, and the demons of the *Chrestianoi,* who might well reach up through the muddy earth and pull me down into that underworld of fire and torment the *Chrestianoi* supposedly believe in.

We proceeded to the mouth of a cave, where a rude tent had been set up, as if to extend the cave mouth out among the tombs. There the *Chrestianoi* seated themselves, on stones or on the bare ground. Some food and wine was passed around. I had heard of this from the prisoners at Nicomedia, the "love feast" of the Christ-followers. It was hardly a feast. We all took a few mouthfuls of whatever was offered, and pretended to give some to the girl Catia, who sat among us as if she had walked in her sleep.

Someone got out—strange as it may seem—a small wooden cross, and reminded those assembled of Christ, who had died on a cross and risen again. Prayers and chants followed, as if to a god. My companions and I mumbled and pretended to follow along. I noticed, to my alarm, that the girl was actually mouthing the words.

Then someone cried out, "Behold! Our prophet comes and brings with him the martyr who has been resurrected!"

There was a flash, like lightning, but *inside the cave.* I don't know what it was, but I smelled a foul, sulfurous smoke. I didn't have time to consider the matter further, because there, illuminated by two uncovered lanterns at the back of the cave, stood the infamous Masked One, who wore a beaten silver mask fashioned like the rising Sun—that is, the rays spread out from the sides and the top, but not the bottom, giving it the overall shape of a fan. He wore a black robe. I couldn't see his hands. Either closely-fitting gloves covered them or he had painted his hands black. The effect was to make the mask seem to float in the air.

Then he began to speak, in a loud, resonant voice.

"I am the foremost disciple of the risen and true Christ, of Jesus of Nazareth, who died, as you know, in Judea in the time of Tiberius, but rose again—and I say to you that on the night he rose he came to *my house* to tell me, first of all those he loved, that he had indeed risen; and he bade me go forth into the world and continue his work, raising up our believers from out of their graves, so that they might never die. I was his *most* intimate friend, the only one to whom he revealed *all* his secrets. Those others who claim to have the truth have but part of it. To me *alone* he revealed the mysteries of the inner light, which is in all of us and in all things, which shines through the flesh and will never die. He said to me, *Lo, I am as the risen sun in glory.*

"Now there is one among us here tonight who has suffered a great loss, whose heart has been torn by the seeming murder of one she loved—"

All eyes turned to us, and to the girl. I froze. Pudens and Catius Magnus looked terrified. Arpocras seemed as expressionless as some ancient, grim statue.

The girl struggled and moaned.

"Yes," said the Masked One, "I can offer you another glimpse of your beloved Charicles. He cannot yet lie in your arms, my dear, for the path back from death is long and hard. Every day I must accompany him for a time on his journey. But you may see him again. Look—"

Another lantern was uncovered. A dark curtain was drawn aside, and there, seated in a niche of stone was a young man, naked but for a strip of cloth about his loins. I could see that he had indeed been crucified. The horrible wounds on his wrists and feet were not healed. His eyes were open. His expression was completely blank. Did anyone else notice that his bare chest did not rise and fall, that he was not breathing?

Did anyone? There were exclamations. The girl writhed and began to moan. The congregation shouted prayers and thanks to their god.

Then the boy began to speak, or at least someone spoke. It was hard to tell. The sound echoed strangely in the little cave.

"Catia," came the voice, *"I long for you. I am coming back to you, my love. Soon we will be in one another's arms forever and ever, and no one can ever separate us—"*

Did *anyone* notice?

Yes, my faithful Arpocras did. Once again we exchanged glances. I gave a signal.

Then many things were happening all at once. The girl broke away from her captors, and staggered forward, screaming. The massive Pudens lumbered forward like a maddened bull and tackled the Masked One, who went down with an audible crunch. Now everyone was screaming. The cultists swarmed over me, wrestling with me as I got out a clay whistle I wore around my neck and blew on it as hard as I could.

Arpocras uncovered his lantern, and light filled the cave. I saw Pudens on top of the still-struggling Masked One, while cultists scrambled over him, like, indeed, dogs attacking a bull in the arena.

Behind him the corpse of the boy Charicles—for corpse it was—toppled out of its niche.

Lighting flashed. Someone hauled me to the ground. Several more swarmed over me, pushing my face down into the mud. I gasped. I was drowning. Then there came thunder, hoofbeats, and the *Chrestianoi* released me and tried to scatter.

There were shouts and screams among the tombs, but soldiers burst out everywhere, and I do not think very many of the culprits escaped.

I stood up, sputtering, as Catius Magnus held onto to his sobbing daughter, and forced her look long and hard at the Masked One, who without his mask was an ordinary, bearded man, his features distorted by pain from a broken leg. And likewise he made her gaze upon the nearly naked corpse of the unfortunate, fanatic Charicles, which Pudens had dragged out into the rain, into the clear light of reason and of Arpocras's lantern.

* * * * * * *

Subsequent investigations, Emperor, were by more orthodox means. It was soon discovered that this Masked One was a Hellenized Egyptian, whose Greek name was Lysimachus. He had become notorious as a fraud and swindler in Alexandria, where he used sleight of hand and various trick effects—indeed he had the ability to disguise his voice or even cast it elsewhere, so that an invisible spirit might seem to be speaking out of the air. Thus he had relieved the gullible Alexandrians of their money until he was finally uncovered and driven away. He fled, then, to his native district in the heart of Egypt, where he consorted with all manner of magicians and scoundrels. He learned from the priests there *some of the secrets of preserving corpses*, at which the Egyptians are so adept. But again, his reputation caught up with him, and he made his way to Asia, appearing in Bithynia under a variety of assumed names, and presenting himself to his followers in a mask, claiming that his face was too holy to look upon and that he was an actual contemporary of Jesus—which would make him more than a hundred years old, unaged, and (so he asserted) immortal.

This much I learned mostly from him during his interrogation, after which he proved quite mortal when I had him executed.

Therefore I am writing to you, Sir, to assure you that *this time* the pestilence of *Chrestianoi* has been eradicated, and that the people of Heracleia Pontica are returning in great numbers to the worship of the gods. Sacrifices are offered, as is proper, before your statue and those of your deified predecessors.

I write, too, to ask of you one more thing, a boon perhaps, though hardly a trivial favor, or even anything for myself. You have instructed me to describe things to you as a friend might, when corresponding with another, not merely as an official reporting to his Emperor. So I have. But as a friend, then, I dare to ask your advice. You have always said to me, "I trust you implicitly. Use your own judgment." But what if I no longer quite trust my own judgment? Catius Magnus is a good and loyal man, and a responsible father. According the law, as laid down by your own instructions, the girl Catia, who, despite everything, persists in proclaiming herself a Christian, should pay the penalty. But this seems unduly cruel to the father, who would suffer much grief. He has already lost his wife, whom he greatly loved, and he has only this girl, however disordered her mind may be, however outrageous her behavior, to remind him of her.

Is there any way she may be spared, even if she must be kept under close watch by her father, so that she may not spread her abominable beliefs to others?

4. *Trajan to Pliny.*

Yes, you may spare the girl, because she has clearly departed from reason, and insane people are not to be held entirely liable for their acts. Furthermore it is good to reward the loyalty of Catius Magnus and to spare him further grief.

5. *Pliny to Trajan.*

Sir, before I left Heracleia Pontica to proceed to Amastris, I gave the news of your merciful decision to Catius Magnus, who was moved to tears of joy and thanksgiving.

I am sorry to report that the girl herself is still insane, though Arpocras holds some hope for her eventual cure. When, in the company of her father, I went to bring the news to the girl herself, she had to be restrained by the two muscular serving-women. Her face was distorted with rage and hatred such as I have never before seen in one so young.

She began to rave and prophesy. She said that one day the *Chrestianoi* would rule the world, that even emperors would bow down before the dead Jesus, and the gods of our country would be overthrown and forgotten, their images broken up into bits and powder.

I repeated to her that her variously named Masked One was a fraud and criminal, who used trickery to deceive, and that her lover was not resurrected. Even now he lay in his family's tomb, beside his father, the virtuous Damon.

Again she spat and cursed, and announced, rather amazingly, that she didn't care about Lysimachus anymore. She knew he was a liar. (On this Arpocras hangs his hope of her recovery, for her reason is not entirely absent.) Indeed she felt no sympathy for him at all.

"He will burn in Hell," she said, "along with all unbelievers and others like him—" Here she used a word I did not know. "—like all *heretics*."

I can tell you that he burned as he left this world. I ordered his body cremated and his ashes scattered. He did not rise again.

THE STOLEN VENUS
(From the Previously Unpublished Correspondence of the Younger Pliny)

1. Pliny to the Emperor Trajan

You have asked me, Sir, to keep you informed of my progress through the province of Bithynia as I might write to a friend, rather than merely as an official might report to his emperor, and so I shall be, as requested, fulsome in the details.

Having concluded our business in Heracleia Pontica, my party has turned inland, toward Claudiopolis, where there is much to occupy my attention: accounts in arrears and possible civil disturbances.

Unfavorable winds prevent us from sailing up the local river (Sangarius), and so we proceed over rough roads by carriage. The heat oppresses us. My assistant, Servilius Pudens, became ill for a time, but my Greek physician, Arpocras, yet again proved himself invaluable....

2. Trajan to Pliny

Your own well-being, my dear Pliny, and that of your party remain foremost in my thoughts. I am glad that the invaluable Arpocras has cured Pudens of his illness. You are wise to adapt your travel to local conditions. Report to me in detail what you find in Claudiopolis, as the disturbances there have the potential of creating a greater danger.

3. Pliny to Trajan

...It begins with two crows.

I call them my two crows, from the way they squawk at one another. Servilius Pudens and Arpocras (whose name means "Crow" in Greek, I remind myself) remain the best of friends, despite their constant arguments about anything and everything. At times this even resembles genuine philosophical debate, and might occasionally produce a flash of wisdom, like a spark from an anvil.

As we three lay back in our carriage, bumping over the hot, dusty roads, and the subject of current contention was whether or not each of us resembles, either in his name or person, some kind of animal. Indeed, Arpocras, the Crow, is a thin, beak-nosed man whose hair was once dark, while Pudens, so said the Greek in a jesting mood, more resembles a *walrus,* a fabulous, flabby beast reputed to inhabit northern seas; which is ridiculous, and maybe even insulting, as Pudens more resembles a somewhat over-fed but still quite formidable bull.

I might have put a stop to this, but I dozed off instead, and when I awoke the conversation had somehow turned to theology.

"Are you saying, then, Greek"—Pudens put a sneer into that word, which he would not have done if they were not friends—"that the forms of the gods and goddesses do not matter, and Mars does not look like a warrior and Venus does not look like, well, Venus?"

"I suggest," said Arpocras slowly, as if explaining something to a dull-witted schoolboy, "that the true forms of the gods are ineffable, incomprehensible, not something which can be imitated by human art. Therefore, when the sculptor carves a statue of Venus, the goddess may inspire him, but the result exists for the benefit of mankind, as a focus of devotion, but not as a literal representation."

Pudens rummaged about and produced an apple and a small knife. He cut a slice out of the apple, ate it, then contemplated the apple. "You're saying then that if I carve this apple into a face and call it a goddess, it's just as valid a statue by Phidias?"

The Greek snatched the apple and the knife before the astonished Pudens could react, cut the apple in half, then impaled both pieces on the blade, and handed the result back to him.

"Theoretically, yes, but somehow I doubt that you are inspired by any other than the goddess of food. Now, finish your deity."

Pudens ate the apple.

* * * * * * *

This might have seemed too trivial an incident to report, Sir, but it proved prophetic in more ways than one. Indeed, the question of the forms that divinity might take was much on my mind in the next couple days.

We reached Claudiopolis toward evening, and were of course admitted immediately, despite which we were unable to make our way through the crowded streets because a religious festival was in progress. The city, despite its name, despite its refounding as a colony in the time of the deified Claudius, is of a distinctly *Oriental* character, with many remnants of the culture and way of life that were in place before even the Greeks arrived.

This was made all the more apparent when we came to the intersection of the two main streets of the city and, despite our imperial banners, squadron of cavalry, and large caravan of assistants, staff, and baggage, we had to pause to let the goddess *Venus* pass by. Goddesses outrank imperial envoys in most parts of the world, it would seem.

It was an amazing sight, this festival, which isn't even on our Roman calendar. It was something purely local, a gaudy affair with naked youths and maidens strewing flowers along the way, followed by musicians thundering on drums and blasting with trumpets and rattling cymbals; then came a mass of garlanded priestesses, and, finally a great, gilded car pulled by white oxen, in which rode the goddess herself in the form of an enormous marble image, far taller than a man, in the most barbarous aspect imaginable: a face like a harsh mask, with wide, blank eyes, but the body covered with hundreds of breasts, like udders, and the arms outstretched, as if to bestow blessings or (so it occurred to me) to throttle somebody.

"Love in Claudiopolis must be a very peculiar business," said Pudens as the thing passed.

"Keep your voice down," snapped Arpocras, "lest someone hear you blaspheme."

Pudens put his hand to his ear and shouted, "What?" Indeed it was hard to hear anything over the noise of the crowd, which was quite worked into a frenzy at this point. But if a riot were about to break out, it was clearly prevented by the presence of my troop of soldiers, and by the city watch and city officials, who came to meet us once the procession had passed.

Eventually we found ourselves at the house of L. Licinius Aper, a leading citizen of the town, who had intrigued against several rivals (so I gathered later) for the privilege of hosting us.

I braced myself for what was to follow. It is a ritual that recurs every place I visit, some rich person like this Aper pushing himself to the forefront to introduce himself, shower me with every flattery, boast about his own importance, protest his loyalty to Rome, etc. etc.

They always do this because they want something. Somehow it is always the rich and powerful who are never satisfied.

I of course must be impartial, and deal with local persons of importance, keeping my impressions (at least initially) to myself, but I must admit that I took an almost immediate dislike to L. Licinius Aper. He was a red-faced, balding man a little younger than me, about fifty perhaps, but if anyone resembled the fabled *walrus* it was he, having grown so fat with indulgence that, quite unlike Servilius Pudens, he could hardly bear his own weight. A quartet of burly slaves hauled him about in a chair most of the time.

Nevertheless he was animated, sputtering, a ceaseless fount

of information about the town and its people and their affairs. It is not actually a proverb, but should be, that *a man who cannot stop talking may eventually say something useful.*

When he tried to dismiss Arpocras with a wave of his hand, the Greek stood firm, and so did I, and Licinius Aper, realizing his blunder, graciously invited the *three* of us to bathe and dine with him.

He gave us a tour of the house, making sure that we noticed the images of all the deified emperors among his household gods, and that his statues of the gods and goddesses were of the conventional sort. No thousand-breasted Venuses here.

"I hear they have something like that down in Ephesus," said Servilius Pudens, "Only they call it Diana."

"That is exactly my point, my dear fellow," said Licinius Aper, placing his had on Pudens's shoulder with an audible thump and perhaps too much familiarity, though, to be fair, he was actually *walking* then and may have needed to lean on Pudens for support.

"It is?"

"Yes. The natives apply the names of our divinities to theirs, absurd as they might be, and that raises the question of whether they can really be considered divine at all, or just the fevered imaginings of barbarians."

Arpocras coughed, as if to say he did not like where this conversation was going, but Pudens merely said, "Oh really? My friend and I were discussing something very similar this afternoon."

"Indeed?" said Licinius Aper. "Tell me about it."

Tell him he did, and the loquacious Aper dragged on this discussion for hours, through our bath, well into the dinner that followed, only interrupted by vulgar displays of lewd dancers and mimes and acrobats. There was no doubt that our host was going all out to impress, though I couldn't help but think of the ridiculous freedman in the *Satyricon* of Petronius, written in the time of Nero yet as applicable to the present circumstances. But Licinius Aper was a Roman, a true son of the Tiber and the Seven Hills, as he had not failed to impress upon us, as he continued to impress...and if I may add a further new proverb to my short collection, let me say that *the man who strives so hard to impress may ultimately give an impression other than the one he intended.*

More than once Pudens shot me a glance as if to say how he suffered for the good of Rome, doing his duty, putting up with all this. Arpocras gazed into space, stonily, but remained, I am sure, completely alert. The oddest thing about the whole evening was that at times you might think that Pudens was the object of our host's hospitality, and I, the *legatus propraetore consulari poteste* was almost forgotten. But I bided my time, as did Arpocras, waiting for Licinius Aper to get to the point.

He finally did.

The dancers and mimes were long gone. The dinner had proceeded, literally from eggs to apples, and as we lingered into the late hours over dessert, our host said suddenly, "The men of Juliopolis are my enemies."

I already knew of the rivalry between the two cities, a common enough phenomenon between Greek cities in the East. With the might of Rome to prevent them from actually going to war, they often expressed their enmity in sporting competitions, street riots, and more often than not in ridiculous vanities, each striving to build the grander theatre or aqueduct or temple, which were often unsound, over-budget, and the cause of the very evils which I had come into the province to correct.

I sighed, and thought, *At last.*

I will not repeat everything he said, for, even when he was getting to the point Licinius Aper could be long-winded. The gist of it was—as I understood the undertext of his discourse—that certain wealthy men like himself, *Romans,* as he made sure we were all quite clear about, some of whose families had dwelt in the East since the affairs of the region were settled by Pompey over a hundred and fifty years ago, controlled the local economy, the grain markets, the small manufactures, even the religious pilgrimage trade. He being, of course, a *gentleman,* a member of the local senate, did not sully his hands with actual commerce, but worked through agents and freedmen, as did everyone. He and the senators held the city for Rome, and therefore deserved such rewards as they had reaped (although I was determined that there would be a clear accounting during my stay here), etc. etc. But they had incurred the wrath of the men of Juliopolis, their rivals for exactly the *same* avenues of commerce. The god of Juliopolis had an enormous member, Aper told us, snickering like a schoolboy, and was therefore identified with Priapus and the subject of "disgusting" rites.

What precisely did L. Licinius Aper want from me which he was (even yet) not quite willing to state plainly?

It became clear enough: He wanted me to contrive some sort of criminal charge and remove, or even have put to death, one Clodius Carus, his opposite number in Juliopolis.

"A mere Greek," Aper spat out in genuine repugnance—the first sincere utterance I had heard from him, the rest being like the recital of a bad actor. Arpocras drew breath sharply. Our host had obviously forgotten him entirely.

"Not a Roman at all, despite his Latin name, which he surely stole," Licinius Aper went on, "a wretched provincial scoundrel who desires to destroy my wealth, discredit me in the eyes of the emperor...I am certain, Sirs, that he means to commit some *outrage* very soon. I thank the gods for your fortunate arrival so that you might thwart his evil schemes...."

* * * * * * *

Eventually we escaped Aper's hospitality and retired.

"But of course, of course, you have had a long journey," he babbled on and might have spoken volumes more if our own slaves hadn't closed protectively around us to attend to our needs.

I was able to confer briefly with Pudens and Arpocras.

"What do you think?" I said.

Pudens rolled his eyes heavenward as if he were about to

faint, then laughed softly.

Arpocras said, "Did you mark how he said *'my enemies'* and *'my wealth?'*"

"I did. This is some selfish, petty matter, then, not of larger political import—"

"It could be both, Sir."

Verily possibly he, too, spoke prophetically.

I had barely gotten to sleep when the cries of the "outrage" were upon us. There was a great commotion outside in the street. Someone was pounding on the front door. Our host's slaves were up and about, and then so were Arpocras, Pudens, and myself. We had barely emerged from our rooms when an obviously aroused and possibly frightened Licinius Aper lumbered upon us, blubbering, wringing his hands.

"It is as I predicted, Sirs. I fear that it is. An *outrage.* A *blasphemy!* It is the work of my enemy, I am sure, to discredit and destroy our city—"

For the first time he said *our* rather than *my*, as if the catastrophe, for the first time, applied to more than himself.

"What *has* happened?" Servilius Pudens demanded, speaking for all of us.

"It's so—so—incredible—!"

Licinius Aper could have gone on for enough to fill twenty pages without saying anything, if I were to report his speech exactly, so I must condense his matter: it seemed that the goddess Venus of the thousand breasts, the very one we had let pass in the street upon our entry to the city, had *vanished.*

"But that's absurd," said Arpocras. "Half-ton marble goddesses don't just *disappear!*"

Aper leaned forward, as if to deliver his lines in a bad stage-whisper, "They say that she *walked.* The temple suddenly filled with an unnatural light. She struck down her priestesses, and *walked* out of the temple, into the night! The people are terrified, Noble Sirs, as you can well imagine. For myself, I don't know what to think—"

"But you think it might have something to do with the

schemes of your enemy, Clodius Carus," I said, attempting to organize *his* thoughts.

He stopped, startled, as if the idea had not occurred to him. If so, he was stupider than he looked. If not, his acting was getting better.

"We are men of the world," I said. "We don't really believe that *barbarous,* provincial marble statues get up and walk, do we?"

"No, but—"

"Then it must be the doings of this Clodius Carus, yes?"

Suddenly Aper's distraught features seemed *so* much more calm.

"I am relieved that you see that," he said.

* * * * * * *

But first we had to inspect the scene of the crime, and crime it was, too. We all quickly dressed. The centurion of my guards came to report. Accompanied by a troop of soldiers, marching in step, the steady tread of their hobnailed boots imposing some sort of *order* on the chaotic night, we followed them through the streets of the city. Pudens, Arpocras, and I walked. Licinius Aper rode in his chair.

The streets were filled with disorderly people, who melted away as we approached, or just stood staring, silently, as we passed.

We came to the temple, which was of moderate size, Greek in form, but more ornately decorated in the Oriental style.

As soon as I entered, I saw that a serious crime had indeed been committed. There were three dead women, two on the floor, one lying halfway out onto the steps. Their skulls were crushed. There was blood everywhere. These are the priestesses of this Claudiopolitan Venus, allegedly struck down by their goddess when she deserted the city.

And she had deserted it. The thousand-breasted divinity was distinctly missing from her shrine within. The place was filled with thick, strange-smelling smoke. It was clear enough to me that some kind of oil had been set afire on the floor, but this did not burn down the temple because the building was made entirely of stone and the oil was swiftly consumed. I held the edge of my toga up over my nose to avoid choking on the fumes, made my way to the back and examined the hole in the floor, behind the altar, where the divinity had been affixed. It was clear enough to me, and to Arpocras, who stood beside me, that the goddess was shaped out of a single pillar of marble, that she was, when not parading about the city in her gilded car, affixed here like a post, and her walking out of the temple was made all the less plausible by her not having any legs.

"It is shocking! Shocking!" said Licinius Aper, when we emerged from the temple. He had just arrived, and had not ventured to climb the temple steps, though he stood supported by two of his muscular slaves. He waved a hand about, indicating a huddle of glum-faced individuals whom I took to be local senators. "It will be the ruin of us all!"

I am not sure if he was performing for me or for his colleagues, but for once he was telling the honest truth. If the goddess were not recovered, it would be the ruin of Claudiopolis, the end of the religious trade, and much else, as the superstitious multitudes fled elsewhere to avoid a place obviously shunned by the very gods. No one seemed much concerned about the dead priestesses, but financial catastrophe on the horizon perturbed them very much.

I realized it was dawn. After a long day's traveling, a tedious dinner, and these late-hour dramatics, I simply had to call things to a halt. I am afraid my Roman fortitude was giving way to age. I left Arpocras and the centurion in charge and withdrew.

* * * * * * *

In the days that followed I continued to reside in the house of Licinius Aper, as it was the largest and most luxurious in the town, and nothing less would befit the dignity of my office, for all I, personally, would have been content with a comfortable, quiet room somewhere.

I worked very hard. I got very little sleep. It was not merely because Licinius Aper had a habit of bursting in on me at any hour that pleased, offering suggestions, more than once demanding to know if I had arrested "that blasphemous fiend, Clodius Carus."

I reminded him that I was the imperial *legatus* here, and I would give the orders for arrests. I assured him that investigations were proceeding.

"But it's so obvious, *obvious*," he sputtered, wringing his meaty hands as he left.

Perhaps he was trying to distract me from my more expected duties, for he and his colleagues could not have been comfortable about what I was doing. As more and more of the town records were brought to me, it was clear that temples and bridges and the new theatre cost three times what they should have, that some projects accounted for had not even been built. When I went out one afternoon to see the famous theatre, I concluded that it would *never* be completed, because the ground had not been surveyed, some of the walls were already sinking into soft earth, and the whole place was likely to collapse before it was opened. I also found evidence that persons convicted of serious crimes had managed to have their sentences erased, or even transferred to others, for the payment of a suitable bribe. In short, my host and all his colleagues were clearly, as the popular expression has it, lining their togas with municipal gold. There were going to be some prosecutions here, quite aside from the matter of the dead priestesses and the missing goddess.

As for that, Pudens quickly came to the conclusion that the goddess had not, precisely, *walked*—whether or not she actually had legs was not the point.

He spoke in a whisper, lest some of our host's servants might be eavesdropping. We were having this conversation in the central courtyard of the house, where a chair and table had been set up for me in the garden, so I could work comfortably by daylight.

"I think friend Licinius Aper stole the goddess himself."

"But how?"

"Those muscular slaves of his."

"Just four of them?" said Arpocras. "Even for them, that's a heavy statue."

"Maybe they come in matched sets. If he has three quartets, they could have done it."

"They could have just wheeled her off in her car," I suggested.

"I looked into that, Sir," said Arpocras. "The car is in its shed behind the temple. It is not missing."

"But why would he do it?" I asked. "Why would he ruin his own city—and his own income?"

"Isn't that obvious?" said Pudens. "So he could blame it on the men of the rival city, Juliopolis. He'd like nothing more than you to march in there with a legion, knock the place down, and crucify the entire population, starting with this—this—"

"Clodius Carus," said Arpocras.

"Yes. His enemy. It all makes sense. The structure of the explanation is complete and perfectly logical."

"Now all you have to account for is the supernatural manifestations, the noises, the miraculous light," said Arpocras, "not to mention the murdered priestesses. The town is quite full of stories, if you care to go out and hear them."

"I could hardly—"

Indeed he could hardly mix inconspicuously with the local populace, a large, tall, pale Roman. But Arpocras, a Greek, could.

"Nevertheless I can explain those things," said Pudens.

"Do so."

"Aper's henchmen killed the priestesses—bludgeoned them—then carried off the statue, perhaps in an ordinary wagon filled with straw. Well *after* the deed was done, but before it was discovered, some of them set the oil and incense on fire, then rushed out into the city to spread the alarm. Rumor and panic took care of the rest."

Arpocras looked up at him and smiled. "Very good. I see I have been able to teach you some of my methods," he said. "Logical, yes. Complete, yes, as far as it goes. But is it *everything*? Maybe it requires a few flourishes and decorations in the Oriental fashion."

* * * * * * *

It was Arpocras who provided most of the final flourishes. But not all of them.

It was he, too, who suggested, more by subtle hints than by stating it outright, that I might be in actual *danger,* since no one knew what a man like Licinius Aper might do if sufficiently desperate. If I found sufficient evidence to convict him of a crime, what further crime might he—or some of his colleagues—attempt to protect themselves?

But if I were move out of Aper's house, refusing his hospitality, wouldn't that bring about a final crisis?

Arpocras insisted that we must seize the initiative. As always, he was right.

I consulted with my centurion. Most of the soldiers were quartered elsewhere, their function being to protect my party as we journeyed across the countryside, not against sedition inside a friendly city. But at the same time, if the centurion came daily to confer with me on official business, there was nothing Aper could do. I waved him out of earshot. The emperor's business is mine and the emperor's and not his. He could not pretend otherwise.

Therefore I announced one day that my party and the guards were going outside the city to see the much-discussed, overpriced aqueduct. Licinius Aper offered to accompany me, "for the pleasure of the journey," he said in that oily, completely unconvincing stage-manner of his. With hopefully more politeness and perhaps better acting skills, I forbade this, out of gracious concern for his health, the heat of the day, the roughness of the roads—and I didn't mention his girth even once.

He looked unhappy, but we left, Pudens, Arpocras and myself in our carriage, the soldiers on horseback, some of our secretarial staff following in a cart.

We went out to the aqueduct, about which I shall report in detail in another letter. It is indeed overpriced and defective. We inspected it thoroughly, deliberately taking our time doing so. Then, late in the afternoon, after a pause for a rest in the shade of some trees, we made our way back.

Before we reached Claudiopolis, however, a man, who had been waiting by the side of the road, got up and began jogging alongside the carriage. One of the soldiers made to interfere, but I waved him away and Arpocras caught the fellow by the wrist and hauled him aboard.

The newcomer was a short, wiry Greek, a little younger than Arpocras, though, his hair mostly still dark. If I may trust my instincts, there was something about this man, too, like Licinius Aper when I first met him, that I did not like. If Arpocras was my Greek crow, this fellow was more of a vulture.

Arpocras introduced him as a certain Theon. My Greek had wandered about the city for some days, mixing in low places, jangling purses of money in exchange for information, and now, as the climax of his efforts, we enjoyed the company of this Theon.

He was, to be blunt, an informer. When Arpocras dangled a another purse of coins in front of him, he became most loquacious about the sins of Licinius Aper, which he enumerated in more detail than I could remember, although Arpocras was taking notes. But then I bade him get to the point and tell me where the stolen Venus was.

"In the house of Aper, of course," he said.

"But I have been staying in Aper's house."

"He has more than one house, Sir. Surely you knew that? A man as rich as him, you'd expect it."

Arpocras nodded. It was so. Unsurprisingly, Licinius Aper had invested much of his wealth in several houses, which he rented out, and a few farms, which he worked profitably, but the place of interest was a villa he had up in the hills, a little beyond the city, to which he normally retired to escape the summer weather. He had only remained in his city house, out of season, because he knew I was coming, and would have to reside in the city to do my work.

Theon wanted to leave, but I wouldn't let him. The centurion had his instructions. The informant held onto his bag of money, but otherwise sat in the carriage glumly.

We returned to the city-house of Licinius Aper, but the horsemen did not dismount, nor did I get out of the carriage. I sent one of the secretaries in to fetch him. When he emerged, I leaned out between the curtains of the carriage—it would not do to let him see our informant—and told him where we were going. I suggested he come with us.

He pleaded his health, the heat, the roughness of the road.

"Nevertheless, I think you should come," I said.

There was nothing he could do. He followed in his own carriage, driven by one of his burly slaves. And so the whole company, carriages, carts, the troop of mounted soldiers, would through the town and up into the hills, where, after a time, it was indeed cooler. A pleasant breeze blew. It was nearly sunset by the time we reached the villa. Under other circumstances, I might have appreciated the view or even written a poem about it.

But not now. My mind was turning. The last pieces of the puzzle were coming into place. Pudens, Arpocras, and I had all sat in silence during the journey, each of us thinking. I exchanged glances with my colleagues, but none of us wanted to say anything in front of Theon.

We burst into the house without formalities, leaving the porter and the household slaves fluttering, trying to make excuses to their master.

"This is an *imposition,*" Licinius Aper protested. "After all my hospitality, all my kindnesses, is this how you repay me?"

"I *believe* something which I hope is wrong," I replied. "I sincerely hope I am misinformed. If I am, someone will pay, and I will give you my profoundest apologies."

"Well, then, let's go back to the city and discuss this over dinner like gentlemen, shall we?"

Instead I proceeded to a certain room. The door was locked.

"There's nothing in there." said Aper. "That room is not in use."

I nodded, and some of the soldiers forced the door.

It was a large, high-ceilinged room, with murals on the walls. It might have been an extra dining room, or even a bedroom, but there was no furniture in it now, and it was, indeed, not in use.

The thousand-breasted Venus leaned against the back wall, propped up rather precariously, her arms reaching out toward us. Now that I saw it up close, it was, indeed, a deeply alien thing, a frightful image, really, of perhaps great antiquity. It had, indeed, no legs. Breasts like udders covered the whole body, front and back, but for the arms and the fierce, mask-like face. It was, I would guess, about ten feet tall.

Some of those present let out cries of amazement. A couple of the Aper's servants tried to run, but soldiers caught them. Pudens, Arpocras, and I all looked at one another, as if to say, *it is as I thought,* even if, very likely, some of our theories differed.

But before any of us could congratulate one another, Licinius Aper put on the most amazing performance of his otherwise unconvincing career. He *knelt* before the goddess. He *beseeched* her forgiveness. For all he purported to despise barbaric images, I think he was afraid. I think he saw the workings of supernatural providence in this. I think that, far more than anyone else, he was *utterly and genuinely astonished* to find her here.

All of my theories collapsed at that point. I was at a loss. But before I could say anything or do anything, the whole scene came to its dreadful climax. I don't know if Licinius Aper had somehow bumped against the statue, or if his massive bulk dropping down before it had shaken it from its doubtful balance, or if there was another, less explicable cause, but so quickly that no one could react, stone began to grind and the goddess *moved.* She fell forward, her marble arms reaching out to embrace Licinius Aper, her awful face bending down to kiss him—or to devour him.

The statue crashed to earth. There came more cries of amazement and horror. Several people ran from the room and no one stopped them. In the eyes of the Greeks, I am sure, the goddess had taken her vengeance. All I can say is that there was a lot of blood, both arms and the head broke off, and marble breasts scattered all over the floor.

I too wanted to run away, but I remained steadfast. Even Arpocras looked on speechless, as did Pudens. I was the one who managed to tell the centurion to bring the informer Theon in to see what had happened, and when he did, as Theon reacted, the chain of events almost began to make sense again. Almost but not quite. There were still huge and mysterious gaps.

Theon rejoiced. He laughed. He virtually danced for joy, and once more launched into a vast recital of the sins of Licinius Aper, which only stopped when I broke in and said, "I arrest you, *Clodius Carus,* on some charge or other. I am sure I will think of something."

He babbled in protest as the soldiers grabbed him. I turned from the horrible scene and hurried away.

Arpocras ran after me. I have never seen him so flustered. I think what amazed him the most was that for once I'd thought of something he had not.

"But...how did you know it was Carus?"

"He and Aper were two of a kind. Who else would know so much about a man's misdeeds, and be so eager to relate them, except his mortal enemy? Aper and Carus had this fault in common. *They both talked too much."*

* * * * * * *

These events did not settle the puzzling affair, Most Noble Emperor, not entirely.

Since Clodius Carus was not a Roman citizen, I could have him interrogated locally. I am told he became incoherent under torture, but there was evidence of sufficient crimes that I had him executed.

Yet the enigma remains. There are three explanations at which one might grasp: the first that Licinius Aper stole the goddess, hid it in his country villa, and merely put on a last, desperate performance for us when his enemy, who had learned of it, exposed him. But I reject this. He was *too convincing* at the end. He wore his lies like a badly-fashioned mask. I think he was sincerely astonished and even terrified to see the goddess there.

Or could it be that the fatally-loquacious Clodius Carus stole the goddess, placed it in Aper's villa with the connivance of corrupted slaves, in order to destroy his enemy? The image actually crushing Aper was an accident, but the result was the same. This, indeed, is what both Servilius Pudens and Arpocras think happened.

The people of Claudiopolis cling to a third view, which sometimes, toward which, in unguarded moments, I lean myself: that Aper stole the goddess, hid her elsewhere, *and she came of her own accord* to deliver her vengeance.

* * * * * * *

I write to you then, Sir, with a specific question.

Something has to be put back into the temple, to restore the religious commerce of the city. Was Arpocras correct, that the true forms of divinities may never be apprehended by human senses, and that consequently *all* such images, however grotesque they might seem to Roman eyes, are equally sacred? Should I take this opportunity to install a proper, Roman Venus in the temple, or should I employ a local craftsman to recreate the goddess in her original form?

4. *Trajan to Pliny*

You should restore the goddess in her original form, to which the Bithynians are accustomed. It would certainly be out of keeping with the spirit of our age to demand such a change in immemorial religious usage.

Very likely, your wise Arpocras is correct. Certainly the gods and goddesses work through human agencies in mysterious ways. No one can deny that.

LAST THINGS

I can't tell you how immensely pleased I was, though not really surprised, to see that the house of Plautia Marcella stood as it always had, nestled among trees on a ledge above a stream and a narrow valley, in the foothills of the Alps. Throughout my journey I had noted the general impoverishment of the countryside, the very few, stick-thin tenants still laboring in the fields, the burnt villages, the tracts of waste, but here, as my carriage inched across the ancient stone bridge and I gazed up through the dusk at the welcoming villa, time seemed to have never passed. Here was a place immune to the ravages and follies of men and the death-throes of empires. The sight was more comforting than I can put into words.

I had been a guest here many times in my youth, in the old days, when the third Valentinian wore the purple and Roman political fictions went on as they always had, like a stately dance of shadows. Here there was light. Here were solid things. The great lady Marcella's husband had grown greater still in the imperial service, leaving her richer than dreams of avarice—and I think she had few of those, desiring only to live in the old way, without hindrance.

So, in her house, you might think that Trajan still ruled. Some *genius* hovered above the place, a guardian spirit who insured that the life of Plautia Marcella remained like the unrippled water in a tranquil pool.

She would survive, I used to believe, until the end of time, until the deaths of the gods.

But aren't the gods already dead? Ah, I digress.

Suffice it to say that inside this house, strict decorum was always observed. A gentleman wore a toga, never daring to appear in the actually more practical Germanic trousers the twit Valentinian once tried to outlaw. ("A few more attempts like that, and I shall actually believe he is alive, not a stuffed dummy," Lady Plautia once said, but softly, because in those days the emperor's mother, the Christian gorgon Galla Placidia, was still among us, and everything was said softly.) There one spoke perfect, classical Latin, rife with allusions. The eunuch-chamberlain John greeted one at the door. He was a dark, frail little thing, an Armenian with an whispering voice, whose beardless condition made him seem forever a child. It was his task to exchange initial pleasantries and small gifts to and from his mistress, then conduct the guests to the baths, where we would linger in sumptuous luxury, often accompanied by music, sometimes John himself on a lyre or pipe. And at last, at the appointed hour, one followed John and the other servants in stately procession into the triclinium, the dining hall, where Plautia Marcella held her court and the games (of wit and eloquence) were about to begin.

In those days, when I was fourteen or fifteen, I was the best friend of her favorite nephew Sabellianus. For all that I should have felt smothered in such company and been more interested, as Sabellianus was, in hunting or riding, I genuinely liked her. The very artificiality of her condition appealed to my already ripening cynicism. Here was a lady who had *style*.

I was a would-be poet then, spinning vast tapestries of word-play and rhetoric, and if, sometimes, I lost all sense of what I was trying to say in the process, Plautia Marcella always praised my compositions. She too was a cynic, not in any strict philosophical sense, but someone who accepted mere surfaces and did not peer underneath, because she already knew there was nothing there.

Laughter, I associate with her, and very faint mockery, like the wind under the eaves. I could mock Virgil merely by not being Virgil. She could mock Galla Placidia by not being empress.

We became confidants. She was of a far higher social rank than I, which removed any sense of competition. There was no danger I would ever be asked to marry her daughter, Plautilla, who had the potential of becoming another gorgon. So she told me things she told no one else, particularly after my boyhood friendship with Sabellianus had ended, and he had gone off to become a priest and convert the heathen who were arriving across the Rhine in inexhaustible waves. I still visited. We two, together, had our little jokes and our secrets. But there was no possibility of scandal between us. She did not lust after me. She called me one of her puppies.

Once, when only John was present, she said to me, "I have seen the goddess Hecate, walking in my garden with her two black hounds."

That startled me. I said nothing. She waited for my response, but when I did not laugh, or ask if the hounds had left muddy prints or worse on the garden path, she smiled mysteriously, and the three of us rose and went out into the garden, which spread over a series of terraces behind the house. There John unearthed a small stone altar and the three of us, just for the fun of it I think, committed a capital crime. We sacrificed, pouring a little wine over the stone. It was evening, dark very suddenly and the wind blew through the trees. Lady Plautia spoke of spirits, of *daemones,* which haunt every fold of the earth, whether the established Church likes it or not. She conversed with invisible gods as if they were her dinner guests. I could almost see them. The wind blew. The moon was covered with a cloud, and Hecate, goddess of the dead and of witchcraft walked nearby.

I did not even suggest to myself that the lady was mad. No, this was a performance, for my sake. I found it thrilling.

Later that night, in my chamber, I actually wrote a good poem.

Now that I am old and tell this story, I still wonder what, actually, Plautia Marcella believed. Certainly she worshipped

Christ and even endowed a little church once, professing, as everyone did, that in the crucified Nazarene, Rome had found a powerful new ally. After all, she pointed out, the cross on which He died was now on the money, or else the christogram, the chi-rho, depicted on many imperial reverses as being inscribed by a winged victory—which already the vulgar called an angel—onto a shield. So if the penniless carpenter, who did not even own the robe He wore, now found His way onto the golden *solidus* of Rome and those *solidi* found their way into the purses of silken-robed churchmen, then clearly even God was moving up in the world.

But what did she believe? Did she, as I strove to, achieve the placidity of a still, secret pool by believing in nothing at all?

She believed in enough to write to me, without any elegant flourishes, *Come at once. I need you.*

It had begun to rain by the time my carriage reached the house. I ran to the door and knocked. There was no answer, but the door was unbarred, so in breach of all etiquette, I let myself in and stood dripping in the semi-darkness of the familiar atrium. A single lamp hung flickering from a stand. The room was filled with huge shadows. I could see, though, that the niches in the walls for the household gods were filled, as always, with flower-pots, though the flowers seemed to be dead. The floor at my feet was muddy and wet. It would never have been so in the old days.

How long had it been? Twenty years? In the meantime Attila and his Huns had come and gone. The savior of Rome, the supreme commander Aetius, died at the actual hand of Valentinian, who no longer had his gorgon mother around to prevent such a rash deed. Lady Plautia's husband, who had been a partisan of Aetius, perished soon thereafter, as did Valentinian and several of his successors, set up and knocked down like gaming-pieces by the barbarian who had taken Aetius's place, the formidable Count Ricimer. Rome was sacked twice more. Even Ricimer could not save it. The government cowered in Ravenna. People said the world was coming to an end. But the house of Plautia Marcella was still here, eternal, although the floor was dirty.

Somehow I began to find less comfort in mere survival.

I started at a sound. Another light flickered and drew near, and I saw that it was the lady's chief servant John, who had grown white-haired and wizened, his head bobbing atop his thin neck like autumn's last leaf clinging to a twig.

His dark eyes sparkled as before.

"Ah, welcome young master Titus."

No mention of my own long list of pompous political titles. Here I was still Young Master Titus. I bowed.

"Greetings to you and your lady."

The eunuch jerked his head back, like a startled peacock, and his half-smile vanished. "Yes, from my lady." Then he did something which puzzled me. He crossed himself.

I hadn't time to ponder what it meant. I took care of the preliminaries, making sure that my horses and my own servants were cared for. Two other servants I didn't know, both of them elderly, shuffled off to carry out John's instructions. Then we proceeded.

There was no ritual bath. I wiped my wet face and hair with a towel. John offered me a fresh toga, fussing over me to make me presentable, as if I were still a child.

Then, without further ado, he ushered me into the dining room where the Lady Plautia Marcella waited like the timeless Sphinx among her pillows, her powdered face framed by the towering curls of an archaic wig, her eyes still alive behind it all as if she were peering out through a mask of stone.

Her brocaded gown rustled as she shifted herself slightly. Then, another surprise. She fingered a golden cross she wore around her neck. She seemed, I thought, distracted and even afraid.

I bowed and she nodded.

"So you dropped everything and came. I am deeply touched."

I did not trouble her with the news that all discipline was breaking down in the City, crimes went unprosecuted, the law courts too often addressed empty air, and if one of the assistants to the urban prefect disappeared for a few weeks, no one would much notice.

"I wish I had the time to keep up a proper correspondence."

She clutched her cross and made a bony, spotted fist. Her wrist shook, and her face twitched slightly, uncontrollably, reminding me that for all her facade, she was truly ancient, possibly as old as eighty.

She jerked her head and seemed to forget something, then said suddenly, "And what about your poetry? Dear boy, you were going to conquer the world with poetry, once upon a time."

I shook my head sadly, both amused and melancholy that I was still her Dear Boy past the age of forty.

"No?" she said. Did I detect a genuine tear?

"Alas, I must leave the poetry to Sidonius Apollinaris. Have you heard of him? I've attended a few of his readings. His work is the perfection of eloquence, and doesn't threaten to mean anything at all."

The lady's face flickered, and for just an instant she seemed her old self. But there was no witty epigram, no wrenching parody of Sidonius's latest, merely a sigh.

"I've always enjoyed you, Titus. I really have."

"And I you, Lady. Truly."

I bowed again. She held out a trembling hand for me to kiss her ring.

Then I took my place on the couch adjoining hers. Two elderly servants came and laid out a simple meal. I observed that they set three places. I raised an eyebrow.

Plautia cleared her throat.

Now I received my third surprise for the evening, more alarming than the other two.

Someone else bellowed in a hoarse voice. "So he's finally here? This isn't a social call you know, just some stupid police business."

Another lady raised herself up on her elbow. She had been lying on the third couch, out of sight. She was red-faced and visibly drunk. She held up her wine-cup for a refill, and one of the servants reached for a pitcher, but Plautia shook her head and he put it down again.

"Mother, you treat me like a child!"

It took me quite a while to convince myself that this really was the once-beautiful, if terrible-tempered Plautilla, daughter of my hostess, half-sister to the now martyred Sabellianus. She had grown stout in middle age. Her beauty was utterly gone. She had been married, I knew, to a certain Valerius Aper, about whom, I knew in my police capacity, no one had ever had anything good to say, save that he was rich. Nor was anything good said about how he spent his money or the way he licked Ricimer's boot-heels until the barbarian finally tired of him and my men found Aper face-down in a sewer with his throat cut.

So here was Plautilla, a widow, living in the house of the widow of a much more honorable man. She had never had patience for anything other than her own whims. She surely felt buried alive.

To me she virtually spat, "You managed to tear yourself away from your pet menagerie of informers and slaves. How very good of you to come."

"Child!" exclaimed Plautia Marcella.

"I *said*, Mother, that I am *not* a child!"

"You are what I say you are. Now greet our guest politely."

Plautilla rose to her feet and waved the cup in an exaggerated salute. "Greetings, oh greetings and more greetings, to the illustrious Titus Vibius Balbinus Pompous Tedious Preposterous whatever-the-hell the rest of your names are, favorite of the gods, lackey of the Cæsars ever since you served as one of Tiberius's little fishies—"

Her mother gasped, genuinely shocked at this reference to an obscenity of four hundred years ago. I was startled that Plautilla was that well-read.

"And now, I think," said the daughter, "I shall take my leave, so you two can chew over old times and rot."

She lurched from the room, first grabbing one of the servants and pointing back at the table. The servant fetched the plate of

Plautilla's food after her.

When she was gone, and the noise of her voice faded, Lady Plautia sighed and said, "Good riddance. Do you think I could get rid of her by marrying her off to the king of the Vandals? It might put some fear of Rome in him."

I said softly, "King Gaiseric is already married, I believe."

"Too bad. How about the king of the Goths?"

"Him too."

She smiled. That was, I think, the very last flicker of her old self that I saw.

Her manner became grave. She dismissed the two servants. John came in and sat down in Plautilla's place. She offered him a few morsels from her own plate, a sign of great honor to a servant.

John looked at me, expectantly.

"The actual reason I have summoned you here, Titus," the lady said, "is that I feel death very near. Now wait, before you start reciting clichés about what a wonderful life I've lead or how death is but the twin of sleep, or the usual poeticisms, or even a remonstrance that someone my age should at least get used to the idea of my own demise, let me explain what I am afraid of. *I am bewitched,* Titus. Someone is trying to murder me by witchcraft. Demons whisper at my window. There are apparitions, portents. It's very clear—"

"But—" I couldn't believe I was hearing this. Not from her. Witchcraft and the gods had been a toys for her, one more subtle joke. Did she actually want me to believe that Hecate walked in the garden? I concluded, with great sorrow, that Plautia's mind had gone soft. For her, senility would be far worse than death, because she would lose her dignity.

Yet she continued, forcefully and coherently, and I deferred judgment.

"I am not afraid to die, of course, if death means that I can rest, but you know perfectly well that the victim of witchcraft does *not* rest. Of that, I am truly afraid. I would be condemned to haunt this place, until the time of the deaths of the gods."

Aren't the gods already dead? I wanted to ask, reverting likewise for the very last time to my own former self. Instead I said, "How can you be certain?"

She seemed very tired all of the sudden, almost unable to speak. She nodded to John. "Tell him."

The eunuch's head bobbed more precariously than ever before. "I found them. The signs."

"Tell him what signs."

"The head of a rat nailed to the door. A bundle of bloody feathers in the Mistress's bedclothes. A mirror with a nail driven through it. And, most recently, her name written in secret places inside her private chambers, each day appearing with one letter removed, diminishing."

"Today there was just the 'P.' I know I shall die very soon."

"And the apparitions?" I asked.

"Yes," said John. "I have seen them."

I wanted to ask more, but events moved too swiftly. The Lady Plautia felt suddenly ill. John hurried her off to bed. It was only half an hour later that he came to me in my room, tearfully and in secret, and whispered that his mistress was dead.

So she was. I followed him at once to her room and beheld her sprawled across the bed. She had tried to get up and had fallen back, and lay staring at the ceiling with an expression the vulgar might take for abject terror. But of course her eyes were merely open, and glassy, rolled up so that only the whites showed. I closed them with her hand. Her mouth hung open, merely slack, of course, because the facial muscles of a dead person lack the energy to hold any expression.

I didn't think she had died of terror, though by the terrified manner of John, he obviously did. More likely, poison. I didn't have time to worry about how much I might have consumed myself at supper. Most likely it had been cumulative, administered on many occasions.

To John, I said, "Does anyone else know of this?"

"Not yet—not yet, Sir. Not yet."

So I was no longer Young Master Titus. All things must pass, in time.

"Then—can you do what I require of you?"

He nodded his head so eagerly I thought it might fall off. Now his manner was that of a child again, a scared child, but, I hoped, an obedient one.

"Good. Give out to the servants that the mistress is ill, but very much alive and ... say that she is delirious, both cursing her daughter and demanding to see her. Say that she commands her daughter's attendance, and that Plautilla must come alone. Then keep everyone in their rooms and away from the corridor outside. Can you do this?"

"Yes, Sir, I can. My poor lady!" He crossed himself.

"Do it for her."

Then he was gone and I knew what I had to do.

Now in my old age, as I tell you this story, I tell you also that it is total disbelief which opens the eyes. The scales fall away. The ugly, unpoetic truth is revealed, all mysteries are unraveled, and even the secrets of the dead and of the gods fail to deceive.

If you believe in nothing, all is light.

I lifted the lady's corpse out of the bed and concealed it, unceremoniously, in a chest half-filled with gowns. She weighed almost nothing. She felt like a bundle of sticks. Then I wrapped one of her gowns about myself and put on her wig, not the towering one she'd worn at dinner, but a smaller one she'd worn to bed. Plautia Marcella was that vain, even in private, even as she'd come to her room in distress. That my hairline had receded past my ears cannot cause much surprise, because I am a man, but she was balding too, and the effect was undeniably hideous. It was something she could not allow. Her whole life had been a matter of things she had not allowed: time passing, decay, the loss of beauty, death by witchcraft. At the very end she had commanded, and the Fates and Furies did not obey. These were her last things.

I merely disguised myself thus, extinguished the lights, and lay beneath the covers, waiting.

I did not have to wait long. When I heard shuffling footsteps outside in the corridor, I rolled over to face the door, so I could watch what followed through half-opened eyes.

When the door opened, I deliberately rustled the bedclothes and let out what I hoped was a convincingly soft moan, so that whoever stood in the doorway and peered into the darkened room would know that the occupant was indeed and perhaps unexpectedly still alive.

I beheld an apparition. A glowing face, wild in its aspect, with eyebrows raised to silvery points floated into the room. The eyes were heavily shadowed, outlined in black. The thing wore a golden tiara in piled, dark hair, to suggest the crescent moon rising in the night sky. (But wait a minute, I thought, isn't that supposed to be Diana who wears the moon, not Hecate?) I discerned, too, a flickering lamp held in one outstretched hand. In the other, a bronze dagger gleamed faintly.

The thick, rustling form swayed around the bed, doing what was perhaps supposed to be a dance, chanting in what might had been bad Greek, or the unknowable language of Olympus, or even the secret speech of the underworld, which is heard only by the shades or by those about to die, and spoken by the dark Goddess of Death.

This goddess was somewhat heavier than those depicted in classical statuary, and smelled of wine.

When the dagger drew near enough, I reached up and seized the wrist of the hand that held it.

The would-be divinity shrieked as I leapt out of the bed. The moon-tiara clanged to the floor. I lost the wig I was wearing. Though my opponent was considerably heavier than I was, I easily wrestled her out of the room and into the corridor, where there were lamps lit in some of the alcoves and I could see what I was doing. I snatched Plautilla's own lantern from her and set it down on a table. "Look at you!" I said. "What did you think you were doing?"

She rolled her eyes and laughed. "Look at *you!* Dressed up in Mama's clothes. I knew you were like that all along."

I let the mistress's nightgown slide from my shoulders, onto the floor.

Plautilla howled and spoke some more of the language of the gods. She wrestled with me, still holding the dagger.

"Fear me!" she said, reverting to ordinary Latin. "Titus, be afraid. I am possessed by the spirit of Hecate!"

I twisted the dagger out of her grasp and slapped her across the face with the back of my hand.

"I should think the Goddess would find a more suitable vehicle to ride in."

Plautilla's resistance ceased. She sobbed. "But you *believe* in these things! Mother certainly did. You should have seen her shiver and shake. She even started saying her prayers like a good, pious Christian. I had to laugh. *But the old mummy wouldn't die.* I couldn't wait forever."

"You thought you would inherit her fortune."

"Who else? What else could the bitch do with it?"

Still holding her by the wrist, I pulled her face close to mine, and said in as vicious a tone as I could manage, "Maybe she was going to endow a home for retired gladiators." I don't think she appreciated my joke, that the gladiators would have to be very old indeed, and very few, since there had been no such performances in Rome in about seventy years.

She spat in my face.

"No goddess would behave thus," I said. "And once it is clear that there is no goddess...you have made no attempt to conceal anything, have you?"

Indeed, there was no labyrinth of clues, no puzzle. Everything was as clear as writing on the walls, the letters diminishing to a single, final truth.

She had concealed nothing. With utter contempt she showed me where she had left more chicken feet bundled above the door, and yet more places where she had traced mysterious sigils and curses on the walls with charcoal. And there were other masks she had worn, to provide other apparitions. There were even two black dogs kept tied up in a shed behind the garden. The poor creatures seemed starving. I unleashed them and let them run.

At the very last, Plautilla showed me the place in the cellars where she had set the skull of a child on an altar and traced signs on it in blood with her finger.

This alone had not been designed for her mother to discover. This alone, she had done in private. I wondered if Plautilla might not be the credulous one, even slightly mad. *What did she believe?*

"So, what are you going to do?" she said. "If this is all rubbish and doesn't have any effect, then how are you going to prove that I murdered my mother? I just did a little show and dance for her. She always wished we could have theatrical entertainments again, like in the old days. So I am innocent of any crime. Let me go. And get out. This is my house now."

I let go of her and picked up the skull. It felt fresh, boiled to make it bare, rather than one from which, over time, the flesh has naturally decayed. Plautilla almost had a point. I could not prove poison. There was a case here for criminal witchcraft, but if Plautilla argued that she did *not* believe in these things, that they were only evidence of a much lesser crime, a sort of fraud, and no heathen gods or demons had been seriously invoked, she might win. She had enough money now to bribe any judge I had ever encountered.

What then?

The skull. It was fresh, the one thing she had too-brazenly flaunted. She had at the very least desecrated a recent grave, or, more likely, murdered some unknown child, perhaps because she truly believed, or merely to make her own performance more convincing.

These matters become so simple when one detail is enough, and you don't have to prove anything more.

But now that the world is coming to an end, there are signs and portents everywhere, and we who do not believe still see them, just like everyone else.

In the morning I conducted Plautilla to my carriage, bound. As I was now serving in my official capacity, I put on the uniform of my office, which included a military helmet and a mailed cuirass. I wore a sword, which clinked and clattered as I walked. I looked up at the house one last time, certain I would never see it again. I wondered if the ghost of its mistress would haunt the place.

In the course of our journey, Plautilla cursed me, sometimes speaking in her supposed supernatural speech, still trying, I think, to awaken some superstitious fear in me. Sometimes she spoke of old times, pretending we had been friends once. It was all I could do not to strike her.

We came to a main road, then to an imperial posting station. In my official capacity, I could draw on supplies here, have my horses looked after, or even get fresh horses if I were in that much of a hurry.

But the German lout in charge laughed when I showed him the badge of my office.

"Haven't you heard?"

Several of his barbarian companions gathered around, snickering.

"Heard what?"

"Your little Augustus has been booted out." The German sashayed, as if to indicate a little girl. "The army in Ravenna killed Orestes the patrician, and his little baby emperor is gone... away." The Germans laughed. Some of them drew their fingers across their throats.

Actually the emperor Romulus was about sixteen at the time, and I later found out that he was not killed, merely sent to live near Naples, but he was indeed the last.

"What's more," the German said, "our general Odoacer decided to make himself king. So there isn't any Roman Empire anymore, and there's no Roman law, and we don't have to obey you."

Again the Germans laughed.

"I think I know what you will obey," I said. I flipped a golden *solidus* onto the counter. It fell reverse side up, with the cross showing.

Later, I unbound Plautilla and let her eat dinner across from me, seated at a table in the German manner. I hoped she found this an unbearable hardship.

"You have to let me go," she said. "You heard what the man said. There's no law anymore. At least none that you represent."

"I ought to kill you then, and it wouldn't be murder."

She almost laughed, but her laughter froze in her throat.

Yet I did not kill her, if only because by doing so my hands would be indelibly soiled.

So I left her there. I gave the Germans a couple more coins and implied that they should do with Plautilla whatever they felt appropriate.

Never mind law and conscience. Thus we are compromised.

Can a soul be damned which does not believe in souls or damnation? A puzzle. A labyrinth. I am without a clue and deduce nothing.

Jesus Christ have mercy.

IN A BYZANTINE GARDEN

She was a very old woman who liked to sit in the sun, in the garden, and listen to the birds. Sometimes she gazed up at the gulls shrieking overhead and wheeling toward the Propontis and imagined that she could follow them, far away, to the Asian shore and beyond. She had never traveled much, not even in her youth, but had spent her whole life confined, in places like this garden, where now she sat, sometimes muttering to herself, possibly in prayer, her servants thought, but they couldn't tell. Sometimes she made odd little sounds to the smaller birds in the bushes, as if in her vast age she had learned the secret of her speech.

Whatever she did, she had to be humored, for she was the *Basilissa,* empress of the Romans, and as such God's regent on Earth.

Her servants stood by, patiently.

Then the footsteps came, and she looked up, bewildered at first, seeing the face before her of someone she had thought long gone away. She remembered a slender, dark-haired boy with dark eyes, with a beguiling smile and a winning manner, someone about whom she had once had fevered and secret dreams. She saw that face peering out from behind wrinkles and sagging flesh as if from behind a mask. The eyes were the same. Yes. She knew the eyes.

"Empress...Majesty...My Lady?" He bowed down.

She recognized the voice too. Now everything was clear to her, as if she had just opened a book, read the first page, and realized that she had read this book before and, in fact, knew it by heart.

She saw that the newcomer had brought with him several attendants. For just an instant she was afraid.

It was her ancient enemy, the Grand Logothete.

Testing his intentions, she motioned that his attendants should leave. He nodded to them, and they left.

She bade him rise and sit on the bench beside her.

He opened a small box and took out a ring. He leaned over—she did not resist—and put the gleaming, jeweled bauble on her finger.

"It is very rare," he said. "From India. It belonged to a great queen once."

She slid the ring off her finger and softly laughed. "Once, I delighted in such things. Now I am too ugly for anything to make beautiful."

"Empress, in my eyes your beauty rivals the Queen of Heaven!"

"Tush! You blaspheme—but you're still good at it."

She glimpsed that old, familiar, utterly disarming smile of his. She wept.

"Empress?"

"I am tired. Why, at the very end, must we still be at each other's throats?"

"Lady?"

"Don't lie to me. You're still good at that too—" She called him by a private, personal name she had not spoken aloud in many years. "You and I have contended for longer than most people have been alive. We played our game. I took your piece. A servant poisoned. You took mine. Another put to the question. Scissors, paper, stone. Some whisper, calumny, rumor fanned like a faint ember until it is time for the fire to rage up. We circle one another, like scorpions in a bottle. But I ask you, at last, why must it still go on?"

"The vanities of the world are like a golden cloak," he said after some reflection, "burdensome, but difficult to put off."

"Surely you and I are closer to Heaven than to the world now." She clasped the ring between her folded hands now, as if in prayer, trembling. "The only gold I care about now is on the angels' wings. I think they have golden wings, just like in the paintings. Don't you?"

"I am certain of it," he said.

"Can't we then put aside our differences—?"

"Lady, I have come to discuss that very matter—"

But they didn't discuss that matter, at least not for a long time. They spoke of small things, of the few times they had sailed together on a boat across the Propontis and had, indeed, touched the Asian shore. He quoted lines from a verse no one had sung in generations. She tried to remember the rest. She recalled more things, known, it seemed, only by two children long dead. They had loved the other, once, long ago, before learning that life is a mask one has to put on and there is only the stately, ritual dance which fills the days of courtier or the *Basilissa*.

She felt like a prisoner, loaded down with many chains, who has a chance, at the very last, to let them drop. To throw away all masks. Couldn't they do this, the two of them? Couldn't they *let go*, declare no one the winner or loser, *just stop?*

For hours they sat side by side. She leaned on his shoulder. Sometimes they spoke. Sometimes they listened to the gulls wheeling toward the Propontis. She was dreaming while awake. Perhaps she dared to hope. He promised her peace, a cessation. In the end they embraced. He kissed her on the lips. She made no protest when, again, he slid the ring onto her withered finger. Before he departed, they prayed together.

"Shall we meet again, here or in Heaven?"

"We can only hope for Heaven, Lady. We are never certain of it."

She almost said something more. She mouthed the words but did not utter them.

Then he was gone.

* * * * * * *

"She is weakening," he said to his men, as soon as he was out of earshot. "It is time for us to bring our designs to fruition."

* * * * * * *

She whispered to one of her servants. "Kill him now."

* * * * * * *

She was a very old woman who liked to sit in the garden and listen to the birds. She'd heard once that an earlier *basileus* had golden, mechanical birds which sat in a golden tree. Deathless, they could sing forever.

THE DEATH OF FALSTAFF

The King was in Southampton that night.

Everyone had left me but the day before: Nym who was once to be my husband, though I had little liking for him, and Bardolph, whose nose glowed like a lantern, and the boy, and even my own Pistol, who was my husband. Off they were, to France, in their country's service, for God and gold and glory, but mostly for the gold, if you take my meaning. Now the tavern was empty and silent, as all those who had made merry in it had gone away, with even my own husband saying, "Sweet Nell is such a clever one. She will take care of everything."

So they left me, even my husband, to clean up after them in more ways than one.

And with poor Sir John still lying in the bed upstairs. It was I who was to attend to that, who would send for the undertaker and clean up the remains of Sir John's life as if I were wiping a tabletop.

Trust Hostess Nell. She can look after things.

A lot more happened on that night than just myself sitting around in the dark mourning for Jack Falstaff, though I shed many a tear, and I sat by him in the dark, I did, looking at his dim shape in the dark, his nose all sharp and his fine, round face shrunken like a winter's apple. I wasn't afraid, being with a dead corpse, because it was only Sir John and I didn't fear his ghost.

"Oh, Sir John," says I, "I hope you're in your green fields now—"

And then there was a thunderous knocking at the door. I let out a cry and dropped my little candle. I groped around and found it, but couldn't relight it, so I felt my way to the door.

Still the thundering, as if to knock the whole house down.

"Anon!" I cried. "Anon!" And to Sir John I says, "If that be the Devil come for your soul, I'll just tell him the tavern is closed and send him away."

But it wasn't the Devil at the door, instead a tall, fierce-looking fellow, richly clad, and beside him a man in arms, who might have been a soldier. I couldn't quite tell in the dark, but the one had on a black coat, like velvet, and the other wore a steel cap on his head and a sword at his side.

"Hostess Quickly?"

"Aye."

"I am called Doctor Peake."

"Well whatever you're called, what is your business?"

"Does the body of Sir John Falstaff lie within this house?"

I could not deny that it did, but before I could have any whys or wherefores, this Peake and his bully-boy brushed me aside and come in. They showed me a paper, which they said was from a Higher Authority, but of course I couldn't read it.

There was something strange. I knew they came not from the watch, or from the sheriff; and the thought hits me like a thunderbolt, *My God! They are from the King!* But why? The King did not love Sir John in the end. He broke his heart, and of that broken heart Sir John died. So what would the King care now?

I did as they bade me. I lit my candle from the embers and led them upstairs, then fetched a lamp when it was called for, and the one in the black coat, he that called himself a doctor, he examined Sir John most closely, peering into his eyes and ears with a kind of glass, poking and touching as if a dead man were not a dead man plain to see.

"He is beyond all physick now," says I, but the doctor just growls and says, "Silence, woman," and goes on with his prodding and poking. The armed man looked at me, then at his master, but his master said nothing more, so I was allowed to stay.

I stood there, in the dark by the door, wringing my hands in silence.

At last he was done, and Doctor Peake said to his man, "It is as I had feared."

I didn't ask him what he feared, other than that Sir John Falstaff was dead, and I didn't understand why he would be afraid of that.

The other fellow nodded and hurried downstairs and out of the house. I heard him galloping off.

"And now, Hostess," said the doctor, "if you will fetch some refreshment while we wait, here's a gold noble for you."

My eyes lit up at that, you can be sure. I snatched the coin before he changed his mind and told him for that price he could have King Solomon's Feast; but he only wanted some wine and some cold mutton and cabbage, downstairs in the common room, of course, for to eat upstairs was to invite Sir John to rise up and ask for some, as he always did enjoy his victuals.

But also, for that amount of money, Doctor Peake wanted other things of me, first my swearing my silence, and then he wanted to know divers things about Sir John, his comings and goings and who he met, especially in the last days of his life.

I told what I knew, how the King had broke Sir John's heart, and how Sir John had called for sack and drank so much you'd think he'd drown in it, and how he ate enough for five huge, fat men. Yet still there was no comfort for him in it. He tried to be merry with his old friends, but he could not.

The doctor waved his hand impatiently.

"Enough of that. Did he meet with other than his usual associates? Did he take any stranger aside and speak in a whisper? Did they mention the names Cambridge, Scroop, and Grey?"

"Why Sir, if they was whispering, how would I know what names was mentioned?"

I saw rage in his face then, a flicker, like lightning far away on a summer night; but he was a hard man, and in control of himself.

"Then there *were* such persons? Agents? Conspirators? Speak plainly, woman! There are those who'd have your tongue out for this!"

I was all a-flustered then, and didn't know what to say, for those were names of great men, the Earl of Cambridge, Lord Scroop of Masham, and...I didn't know who Grey was, but he must have been great too, to keep such company. But when do such quality as those come to an Eastcheap tavern to talk with John Falstaff?

"You *said* there were conspirators—"

"Oh no, Sir, if I may be so bold, Sir. *You* said it. I but asked if they was whispering, how I could hear what was said."

Then the doctor was angry again, for just an instant, and he let out a long sigh, like the wind escaping from a bag, and he says, "I have been told, by one who knows you passing well, that you have a better wit and a more observant eye than one might expect from...your kind. Here's a silver groat if you will but tell me with whom Sir John Falstaff did converse this past week or so."

I snatched the coin quick, but all I could tell him, to be truthful was, "He did go out alone, just before he took sick, and he did say it was to meet an old friend over a matter of some money. 'So you are going to pay what you owe me?' says I. Quoth he, 'What? I owe *you?* After such custom as I have given you? I have brought such honor to your house. You've had a prince under your roof because of me.' Meaning Prince Hal, he did, and God save him who is now our lord the King. But Prince Hal then. I think there was a tear in Sir John's eye then, because his heart was broke, but he had his little joke on me and I got never a shilling. Out he went, and he came back, his face all flushed and red, like Bardolph's nose, and his speech was slurry, so Pistol my husband and the boy that was Sir John's page helped him upstairs. Soon after Sir John was sick, and sooner after dead. That is all I know, Sir, in God's honest truth."

"Then you know enough to have perhaps come to the same conclusion as have I, that Sir John Falstaff's death was not natural, but that he was murdered."

"Jesu Christ have mercy!" I put my hand to my mouth.

"There are definite signs of poison on his body. Now the matter darkens, Mistress Quickly, and your tact is required, for this is *the King's business.*"

I let out another little cry, and for an instant you could have knocked me over with a feather, all a-swoon was I, sorrowful and afraid, for he had said this was the King's *business,* which is very close to the King's *doing,* and Oh, what a terrible thing it had to be, how it must be the very work of the Devil, that Prince Hal, who loved Falstaff, became King Henry the Fifth, who did not, and that King, to save himself the shame of his former life, found it politic to have Sir John *murdered.*

If that were true, I did not want to live.

But no, I could not believe it. I prayed to God and promised to repent my sins, and Sir John's too, if it were not so.

Doctor Peake said nothing to comfort me, but only said we should wait.

"What are we waiting for?"

"For another, who has been sent for."

So we waited.

That was all there was to do. I didn't feel like idle talk, so I busied myself, tidying this and sweeping that, and I put some wood on the fire to give us light. The doctor just sat waiting too, drumming his fingers on my tabletop like the patter of rain.

Then past ten of the clock there came hoofbeats in the street outside, and thunderous knocking again.

I went to the door but the doctor got there first, and he opened the door to let in his armed man, who he'd sent away before, and another, whose face I could not see because of his hooded cloak. I think there were more men in the street outside. I heard metal clank and clink, and heavy footsteps.

The doctor closed the door swiftly.

I could see that the newcomer was a young man, tall and strong. He had a mailed sleeve, and I saw the ring he wore, even in such poor light.

Once more I crossed myself, and repented my sins, lest I die that night.

"Is it true, then?" this stranger asks the doctor.

"Sir John is murdered, My Lord," says the doctor. "There is no doubt of it."

And the other one's voice trembled a little, and he said, "But *why* would someone kill a harmless old clown who couldn't conspire his way out of a cup of sack?" He was speaking from his heart, and that surprised me, and I watched him careful, like.

"Begging your pardon, Lord," says I, and I curtseys. "But if you want to go up and see him—"

It was reckless of me to say anything at all, but I was crazy with fear and grief and my thoughts all a jumble; and all the other things I wanted to ask him I couldn't find the words for, not then.

The hooded man nodded to me politely, as if I were a real lady, and said, "Your pardon, Hostess Quickly."

He held out his hand, and if he had not stopped me I would have knelt down and kissed his ring, though at that instant if I knew why I dared not admit the reason, even to myself.

"Oh no," says he. "If anyone is to ask, say only that you were visited by a gentleman this night, whose name was Henry Le Roi, while the King was in Southampton, preparing for his French war."

The doctor said, "I have purchased her silence, Lord."

"Nell always knew a good bargain, though it is not in her nature to be entirely silent, as I well know," said Sir Le Roi. I didn't ask how he knew. To me he said, "Hostess, if you will lead the way."

So I lit my candle and led them upstairs, the three of them, Sir Le Roi, who still hid his face beneath his hood, and Doctor Peake, and the soldier.

We stood before the bed where Sir John lay. I bethought me that I ought to cover him up, but they'd want to see him, so I did not.

"Poisoned, My Lord," said the doctor.

"Poor old, fat, drunk, rascally fool," said Sir Le Roi. "He once said that sack would be his poison."

"But not here, Sir," I said. "He got no poison here, though he drank overmuch, and did not always pay for it."

"That was in his nature," said Sir Le Roi.

"It would seem he was poisoned elsewhere," said the doctor, "and returned here to die."

"We must discover the murderer then," said Sir Le Roi, "and within but a few hours, too, for I have pressing business, as you well know. *Damn!* But for more time!"

"We can hardly search the whole city in a few hours, Lord. Even if we knew what the criminal looked like."

"We must make him come to us. But how to get word to him? He could be anywhere."

"Likely in his bed at this hour," said the doctor.

"I think not," said Le Roi. "I think not. But let me think further. Let us plan our stratagem...." He began pacing back and forth, clinking and clattering beneath his cloak. "If this rogue wants Sir John dead, and thinks he *is* dead, then he'll feel a sense of relief that the task is completed and the tongue he wanted silenced *is* silenced, and this murderer, being a low fellow, will celebrate his exploit in a low manner. I think he will be in a tavern, with his comrades, saluting the completion of their enterprise. He'll be drinking a toast, which I swear will slake his thirst all the way to the gallows."

"That still does not find him, Lord."

Le Roy stopped suddenly. He struck his hand with his other fist. His ring flashed in the candlelight. "I have it! Imagine the fright the fellow would have if he were to learn that *Sir John Falstaff is not dead!*"

"But Sir," I broke in, amazed, "why there he is, cold and dead as you see. You cannot bring him back!"

Sir Le Roi said softly, "In Arthur's bosom, so I hear—"

"Sir!" I said, much alarmed, wondering if this Le Roy might be the very Devil, who could read my thoughts.

He turned to the doctor, to the soldier, then back to me, as if to include all of us in his council. "Hark you then. Pray to God this works."

To the soldier he said, "Station the men all about the street, out of sight, so our quarry may enter the house but not leave it."

"It shall be done, Lord," said the soldier, and off he went.

To the doctor, he said, "We must conceal ourselves. Where?" He looked about the room. There was a trunk, but barely big enough to hide a boy in it.

He turned to me.

"Mistress Quickly, is there a curtain?"

"What, Sir?"

"A drapery. A hanging of some sort."

Befuddled, I could only say, "There's just the sheets."

"It will have to do. Take you a sheet then, and hang it up on the wall like a curtain, as if to cover a window, for all there's no window there. In the dark, he'll never notice."

"Never notice what, Sir?"

"But do as I instruct you."

I did. The doctor was the taller and helped. I stood on a stool by him, and we two nailed a sheet up at the ceiling, so it hung down behind the bed, like a curtain.

Then Le Roy and the doctor hid behind the sheet.

Now this made no sense at all, and they looked like a couple of lunatics, hiding in the room from a dead man, as if this would conjure up who murdered him. I might have laughed, were I not so afraid. But if these were lunatics they might murder *me* and wrap me up in that sheet, and it was no laughing matter.

Sir Le Roi came out from behind the sheet and directed me downstairs, into the common room. The doctor remained where he was, hidden.

"Mistress," says he, in a low, secret voice, "would you undertake an adventure tonight—for gold?"

"I might," says I, not knowing what he meant.

"Would you do it for love of Jack Falstaff?"

"I would, for I did love him, for he was a most merry

gentleman and a true friend—"

"So did we all love him," says Sir Le Roi beneath his hood. Very much I wanted to push that hood back and see his face, but I dared not.

"We?"

"All who loved him, for who did not love him?"

I couldn't contain myself any longer. Call me a fool, but I broke down into tears and cried like a baby, and I spoke my mind clearly, not caring of the result. "No, Sir, not *all*. First there was the murderer, who did not love him at all. But also there was the King, and God strike me dead for saying so. Prince Hal, who *seemed* to love Jack, did not and proved false to him when he became King, and he broke Jack Falstaff's heart when he turned him away and said he knew him not. And, Sir, it may even be that the King so wanted to quit Jack's company that he made Jack do the quitting—"

"What do you mean?" says he, and his voice was very grim, but my fire was up, and I spoke on.

"I mean that maybe it was the King that caused Sir John to quit this Earth."

There I had said it, and strike me dead.

But it was Sir Le Roi who staggered back as if struck, and he let out a little cry of, "Oh," and then "Oh no," and his voice was trembling and I think he wept. I think I could see just a glint of a tear, by the light of the fire.

He took me by both my shoulders and peered into my eyes out of the darkness of his hood, and said, "Mistress, how could you make so monstrous an accusation? It is treason, you know."

"If I hang for it, I hang for it," says I.

"Upon my honor as a Christian, you shall not hang," says he. His voice stumbled, but then gained strength. "The King is in Southampton tonight, as you well know—"

"I know it, Lord. Getting ready for the wars. My husband Pistol is with him."

"May he prove a good soldier."

I doubted he would, but didn't say so.

"What I mean to say, my dear lady," said Le Roi, "and may I be damned to Hell if I lie, is that I am a close companion of the King, and I know his mind, and I swear to you that the King still loved Jack Falstaff, for all that he, in his office as king, could not keep such company. But he provided him with a purse to buy him drink and keep a roof over his head, and, most assuredly, the King wished the old man *no harm.*" Now he let go of me and began to saw the air with his hands, and pace about, like a hound on a leash, straining to run. Once his hood fell down, but I turned away, and he put it up quick. "What the King desires, more than anything in this world, is that Falstaff be avenged. Therefore Mistress Quickly, justify your name, and go quickly to all the other taverns in the neighborhood—and I have the King's word for it that there are many—and proclaim to all that Jack Falstaff is *alive* and has begun to recover his senses, and speaks in his feverishness certain names. God willing, this will frighten the murderer to coming here to finish his work, and we'll *have* him!"

I gaped in amazement.

"Will you do this, for sweet Jack Falstaff's sake?"

"Oh yes, Lord! I will!"

And I went out, fast as I could, to every other tavern that was open that night. I told it to people in the street too, to anyone and everyone. "It's a miracle!" I shouted. "Jack Falstaff is alive!"

Oh they laughed at me. They asked if Jack had changed his name to Lazarus. Somebody threw beer in my face and said I hadn't drunk enough yet. But I told the story, all excited and breathless like, of how Jack Falstaff had begun to recover from his illness—I didn't say from his poison, for that would have given the game away—and now he was back from Arthur's bosom after all and asking after some rogue who meant him harm.

"What rogue?" says they.

"It's just the fever. He's talking nonsense," says I, "but praise God, he is alive!"

When I was alone again, I cried bitter tears, wishing it were so, though I knew it was not.

And past midnight, when I'd cried and proclaimed my throat sore, and thought to drink a little sack myself for the soothing of it, I returned to my own house.

It was dark when I went in, Sir Le Roi was waiting at the foot of the stairs.

"Is it widely proclaimed?" says he.

"Aye."

"And well done," says he, and he went upstairs to hide behind the curtain.

I soothed my throat, and soothed it a bit more. I sat in the common room, soothing it, and perhaps I slept some, and dreamed of Sir John Falstaff and Prince Hal and the Devil all sitting around that table making merry, like in the old times.

Then there was a light and stealthy rapping at the door.

I up took my candle.

"Who is it?"

"A friend of Falstaff's. He wants to see me. Urgent."

I opened the door a crack. There was a big, ragged man outside, with an evil look to him, no friend of Sir John's that I ever knew.

"Is it true that Falstaff's upstairs and he's recovered?"

"It is, but he is weak and old, and cannot have visitors disturb his rest, so if you will just come back in the morning—"

I had to make myself convincing, for if I'd said, *Sure, come right up and see him,* when I was supposed to be harboring a sick man who'd almost died, the rogue would have smelled a rat, or the rat a rogue, or whichever.

Instead he shoved his shoulder against the door and came crashing in. Quick as a snake he caught me by the hair, gave a good yank, and had a dagger pointed at my throat.

"I think Sir John will see me now," says he.

"You're not his friend," says I.

"Maybe I lied. But he *will* see me. Lead on."

I didn't have to pretend to be afraid, because he could have butchered me like a sheep right there and found his way upstairs by himself, but I led on, and up we went, and he stood by Jack's bedside for just a moment and said, "Sir John Falstaff, Roger the Bear has come to settle an old score," and he plunges his dagger into poor Falstaff's dead heart.

Then I screamed and Sir Le Roi and Doctor Peake jumped out from behind the hanging sheet and there was some scuffling in the dark. Doctor Peake went to the window, threw open the shutters and shouted, but by then Le Roi had wrestled Roger the Bear to the floor and it was all over.

Le Roi's hood came off then and I saw his face clear in the moonlight, the shutters being open. Our eyes met. He seemed to be saying, without any words, *The King still loved Falstaff.* And I knew that it was true.

But I am sworn to say that the King was in Southampton that night, preparing for the war.

And that is all there is to tell, though I do not even know the ending, really, because the house was suddenly filled with armored men and the hauled Roger the Bear away all trussed up like they was hunters that had caught a bear indeed.

I heard someone say, "This is no conspiracy, but some trifling matter of an old insult."

And Sir Le Roi, Henry Le Roi, him that knew the King's mind so well, though the King was in Southampton, said, "My conscience is clear."

I can only tell you what I overheard. that Roger the Bear got his name from his sheer ugliness, though I suppose he was like a wild, murdering beast. He was but a common cut-purse and cut-throat, the low, evil sort of fellow Sir John sometimes kept company with, when it was his humour, and the more his grief it was.

I can tell you that it's the way of things, histories and the doings of kings sometimes all turn on little happenings, or nothing. We is but on this world for a little time, and the leaving of it can be just a chance, like somebody stumbles and hits his head, or there's an old grudge and Sir John dumped a cup of sack over Roger the Bear when he tried to collect some money

Sir John owed. Sometimes the great is small and the small is great, all mixed up, and it doesn't mean anything at all.

Sure, no comet blazed for the passing of Falstaff.

The King was in Southampton that night, as all the world knows.

But I can tell you this, too: that as they dragged Roger the Bear down the stairs and out of my tavern, the armor Henry Le Roi wore beneath his cloak rattled like the thunder of a gathering storm, and just a little while later, that storm broke upon France.

MURDERED BY LOVE

"Do you believe," said the ancient man suddenly, as the fire burned low and the shadows drew on, "that death has an echo? Do you believe it, boy?"

I didn't know what to say. I felt insulted. I was hardly a boy, approaching twenty, and, though maybe to so old a man I looked like one. I was a servant who fancied himself an apprentice; my master was the poet-philosopher Chosroes; I felt quite full of wisdom myself. Yet to this ancient house-guest I could have been a fly on the wall or a doorknob, and he deigned to speak to me. Out of politeness, to avoid a bad report of myself, I responded civilly.

"Do you mean, Sir, like an actual bell, that the ears can hear?"

(We philosophers must define our terms precisely.

The ancient, a physician, I had been told, leaned toward the fire. I crouched down to stir the embers. He dropped his cup, a cheap, earthen thing; but I caught it and saved it from shattering. He sat staring at me, his lips trembling, as if it were a struggle to speak. I put more wood on the fire and refilled his cup with wine.

(I thought to construct a pretty allegory out of the cup, the fire, and the shadows; but not now, not now.)

"The echo of death," said the old man at last, "is indeed Pluto's bell, ringing in Hades, for all of us, to summon our souls, little more than a faint shivering of metal for most of us—but still we hear it—and, for the great, or in extraordinary cases, thundering out great peals which are heard down the years, even centuries, signifying a death which is not easily forgotten—"

"Even as comets blaze for the deaths of kings—"

He ignored my fine, stolen rhetoric and said, "I'm going to tell you a story, boy."

He didn't say why. I could have been that fly, that doorknob.

"It happened in Greece, a long time ago."

"They say there are fairies in Greece."

The old man waved his had impatiently to shut me up. "And in Greece they say there are fairies in Scythia, and Scythia they say there are fairies in Hyperborea. But I only saw men there. There was much talk of gods and omens, but my tale is of men, and women, and of one woman in particular, in whose cries I heard the echo of death for the first time. Maybe she was the instrument of a god, but she was also mortal enough."

* * * * * * *

I was not much younger than you at the time *(the old man began; how old he thought I was, I couldn't quite guess),* though the thought of me as a boy seems as fantastic as any fairy story. But it was a long time ago. Theseus was Duke of Athens. He reigned there with Hippolyta, she who had been queen of the Amazons before Love—and her husband's army—conquered her.

In those days I was a person of low estate. I won't deny it. I was a *slave,* whose task it was to ride hither and thither across the countryside to deliver the potions of the physician Diomedes. Whatever the weather, or time of night, whatever humor I was in, I had to go forth when my master bade me. That this particular night was a foul one, that rain stung my face and I shivered in my flimsy *chiton,* that my bare legs and feet had gone numb clinging to the exhausted, terrified horse—none of these mattered, for the feelings of a slave do not matter, any more than do the feelings of a tool in the hands of a workman.

You don't have time to feel. You merely *do.*

That I was cold and numb and not a very good horseman ultimately did matter. These things led me to disaster. Suddenly, lightning flashed. My horse reared up. I had a glimpse of an appalling apparition in the road—a dead woman walking, her grave wrappings streaming in the wind. Then I was tumbling head over heels, flying through the air. With the resilience of youth I landed unhurt, but was at once terrified, not of the apparition or of the lightning, but of the thought that the jars I was carrying could have been smashed, that my master's precious potions were lost, and I was in for a whipping to be sure.

I groped around in the dark for my satchel.

Lightning flashed again, and again I saw the shrouded woman. She was rummaging through the satchel, hurling this or that aside. I saw her open on intact jar, sniff the contents, and pour them out. Then she wept, and cried, "There is no death in them!"

Darkness closed in, and she was invisible.

In the darkness I heard her say, distinctly. "Palamon." Thunder crashed. I hear one more thing. She said, "Forever in love."

And it seemed that her voice lingered in the darkness for a long time, an echo, only slowly fading away.

I was alone in the rain and the cold, and I could only gather up the shards of the broken bottles, and the empty ones—for she had drained several. I made my way back to my master's house on foot and arrived in after dawn, covered from head to foot with mud. I expected the worst, and, sure enough, there was my master standing at his gate, striking his palm softly with a rod, pacing back and forth.

But he was a fair man. He let me explain myself first, and after I had done so, however incoherently, his manner changed all of the sudden, as if the sun had suddenly burst through a dark cloud; nay, as if a miracle had happened and a god had reached down and touched us both. That's how it seemed. I was on my knees. My master put his rod aside and raised me up. He embraced me fondly, muddy as I was, and called me, not by my slave name, Rider, but by my real name.

"Phraates," he said, "you are my oracle. You have provided the key ingredient, the clue, the solution to a problem which has sorely vexed me. For its solution I have been promised a rich reward. You too shall be rewarded. You have turned the key in the lock, and behold, the chamber is opened and the secret revealed."

I could only say, stupidly, "I have?"

* * * * * * *

The ancient Phraates, the house guest, paused in his narrative. Silently, he sipped from the cup I had saved from destruction. He sat back and closed his eyes. For a moment I thought he had actually gone to sleep. I sat on the floor before him—it would have been presumptuous to share his bench—and fidgeted impatiently, all the while thinking that if he never told me the rest of the story, I could make up the rest myself, a romance, which would bring me fame.

But then his eyes snapped open, and he seemed to be listening to something in the distance. I strained. I heard nothing but his own labored breathing, him hissing between his teeth.

"In death," he said, "the gods often speak to us. By death, the living can be suddenly and irrevocably transformed, cast down, or raised up. So was I."

* * * * * * *

(Phraates resumed his tale.)

Probably to appease some god he embraced me, for he was the sort of man who sacrificed to Zeus before any great undertaking, to Hermes before he went on a land journey, to Poseidon before he went by sea, to Apollo when he sought learning, to Athena for the wisdom to understand what he had learned, to Aesculepius every day, because he was, after all, a physician—probably, for some such obscure reason, though I will not say that he was without compassion, only that masters do not suddenly embrace their slaves like long-lost children any more than carpenters embrace a chisel—a wise master *takes care* of his slaves, even as a carpenter wraps his tools to protect them from rust, out of his own interest, and if the chisel could speak it would be glad for it—but I digress—

Master Diomedes summoned other servants, who hauled me off to the bath, then dressed me in finer clothes than I had ever had before, and tied on the first pair of shoes I had ever worn, and combed and trimmed my hair so I would look presentable, almost like a young gentleman—

I speculate that he did this on the instructions of some god, though I did not see any god, or hear any divine voice.

In any case, I was still a slave, but now my master's assistant, rather than just his delivery boy.

* * * * * * *

Phraates cleared his throat and paused again, seeming to organize his thoughts.

"We go through sudden changes," he said. "The wise man makes the best of them. If you're suddenly lifted up several steps of the ladder, keep on climbing. Don't ask too many questions. Keep your mouth shut."

* * * * * * *

(He resumed his tale.)

I had no time for sleep. I strained to keep awake and attentive as Master Diomedes and I raced through the countryside in his two-wheeled carriage, bouncing over the rough roads, hoofbeats and the wheels clattering.

Sometimes Diomedes had to shout as he explained the circumstances, somewhat.

"Lord Theseus summoned me," he said. "It is a matter

important to the state. A noble warrior, a friend to the state—" (Bump! thwack! The master's head rebounded from the inside of the roof of the carriage.) "...pining away, a mysterious illness. I could find no cure, when it was so obvious. Why didn't I see it before? You have made it all clear to me, Phraates, and for that I am truly grateful."

I thought that for once he truly was. That was another miracle. It was a time of signs and portents and miracles, if you believe in that sort of thing.

We rode. Diomedes told me something of the tale of Palamon, a great and noble warrior, a veritable Ares among men, perfect in courage and chivalry, but originally from Thebes and our country's enemy. (Or his county's. I, a slave, had come from elsewhere in my mother's womb, captive.) This Palamon and his cousin Arcite—also a mighty man of valour, and perfect in courtesy—fought against Athens in the recent war, and were captured.

Diomedes emphasized again and again that these two youths were flawless in every way, like sword-blades newly forged and polished by a master smith. But in prison they rusted, that is to say their souls were corrupted.

"By love," said Diomedes. He spat the word. He, a man of reason, had little use for passion. He might propitiate Aphrodite, but only to get her to leave him alone.

By love were the two brothers undone. In prison, they both spied the beautiful Emilia. "Which one saw her first doesn't really matter, does it, Phraates?" said my master, "but to them it somehow mattered very much, and was the spark that ignited their deadly quarrel. So I suppose this nothing became everything."

Wearily I nodded my head. I meant to agree with him. I held my neck rigid, so I didn't nod again and fall asleep.

Once the two knights were wounded by love, it was all over between them. They struggled to remain true to their own heroic characters, adhering to all the outer forms, but each, basely, lusted after Emilia for himself (so Diomedes told it), for all she was sister to Queen Hippolyta and hardly a chattel. Did they woo her? Did they even let her know how their hearts were breaking for her? Did they ask if she had any feelings for them? Well, no. How could she?

"You'd think, Phraates," said my master, "that the sensible thing would have been for the two of them to confess their problem to the lady and let her decide which she would have, if either, but no—"

We hit another bump. I was nearly hurled from my seat. Diomedes caught hold of me and hauled me back into the speeding carriage, without slowing down. I wanted to ask why we were driving so fast, why my usually reserved master was suddenly in such a hurry, but I did not. Discretion is the better part of exhaustion.

Palamon and Arcite became madmen for love. Now each was the other's foe, unto death. It happened that Arcite was released from prison, and sent into exile, a generous sentence, you'd think, he being a foreigner anyway. If my mother had been exiled back to her own country, I'd never have been born a slave. But Arcite sneaked back in disguise. Meanwhile there was a veritable epidemic of lovers' lunacy. Cupid's arrows were falling like rain. The gaoler's daughter fell hopelessly in love with Palamon, again, it would seem for no reason, merely because she glimpsed him through the prison bars when she brought him his supper, or something like that. Such was her madness that she actually thought that Palamon loved her, and if only he could escape, the two of them could run off together. But she was a drab. What was she next to the incomparable Emilia (who was also the queen's sister, and rich)?

Nevertheless, she let Palamon out of jail, even though it put her own father's life at risk.

Palamon ran off, but without the daughter. He met Arcite in the forest. The two of them tried to settle their differences on the spot, but they made so much noise with their cries and their swords clashing that Duke Theseus's hunting party caught them in the act.

For their capital crimes (Palamon's escape and Arcite's violation of his parole), both could have been beheaded then and there, but Theseus was merciful (or perhaps crafty, or maybe bored and bemused), and he decreed that the two cousins, and assorted companions to assist them, should fight to the death, not in a sordid brawl, but in a proper contest.

Arcite won. Palamon wasn't killed, though, and had to be led to the executioner's block. The axe was actually raised in the air when a messenger suddenly arrived, shouting, "Hold! Hold!" and bringing the incredible news that Arcite was dying.

He had capered about to celebrate his victory, and fallen from his horse. In a last act of breath-taking nobility, reaffirming the goodness of his character, he had surrendered his claim to Emilia, whom he bade Palamon marry.

That was the end of the official story. It is celebrated already in song and romance.

"But the truth, good Phraates," said my master, "may not be so neat. The blade left out to rust, may be a bit tarnished."

Blearily I said, "What happened to the gaoler's daughter ... whatever her name was?"

"Her name does not matter, Phraates, but I see that I chose well to make you my assistant, for you go right to the heart of the matter. The daughter went spectacularly mad, traipsing around the country decked in flowers, singing mad songs. She tried to drown herself, but was rescued. I was called upon to supervise her cure. I did what I thought right. I instructed her own wooer, a lad of her own station who would be a proper husband to her, to call himself Palamon and come to her in the dark. The mad mind is easily deceived."

Somehow I doubted that, but I had enough sense not to argue medicine with the most learned physician in the land. Instead I said, "And what is the matter, that all this is the heart of?"

Now the carriage slowed. We were approaching a humble cottage. The door hung open, I could see. Chickens and sheep wandered randomly in the yard.

"Again you are incisive, Phraates." Diomedes pulled on the

reins. We approached the cottage cautiously. "The high matter of state, on which Duke Theseus consulted me again, is this: Now Palamon is dying. He is now the Duke's valuable ally, and his brother-in-law, and he wastes away from some mysterious, draining sickness which even I cannot cure. Or could not until now, because I had overlooked the obvious cause and source."

"And what is that, Master?"

"You're tired, boy, or you'd know. It is that plague we call Love."

Now Diomedes brought the carriage to a halt. We two got out and walked to the cottage door. From within I could hear the sound of flies buzzing.

Inside was a dead man, sprawled over a table, his throat cut, his blood drained out into a bowl as if he were a sheep. But on the walls, in the murdered man's blood, someone had written: FALSE. FALSE. YOU ARE NOT PALAMON.

Diomedes sighed.

"It is one of love's casualties."

"Who is he?"

"The young man who was to become husband to the gaoler's daughter. Out here, far removed from the scene of her misfortunes, I had hoped, she would recover her reason, and live happily enough with the fellow."

"But the cure didn't work."

"No, Phraates, and now raging Love runs rampaging over the countryside. We must return to Athens."

* * * * * * *

Ancient Phraates grabbed me by the wrist. He squeezed hard, with surprising strength.

"Have you ever been in love, boy?"

I had enjoyed my amours, and thought myself a gallant, but didn't care to discuss such things with this foul-breathed (for so he was) windbag (increasingly), and lied, "No, Sir, not really."

He let wine dribble from his cup into his lap. He didn't seem to notice. "Then you won't be unable to understand, boy, any more than I could at the time. I thought my master was a fool, to have overlooked the obvious. Only later did I understand the depth and profundity of his error, and only a deep thinker can even make such a profound mistake. He was right to despise love, but he should not have underestimated death. It was Pluto's bell, ringing, ringing, and the echo of it resonated out from Arcite's grave, and it drained away Palamon's life, and it made the gaoler's daughter mad—"

At this juncture an owl flew in through an upper window and hooted among the rafters. Another omen. A message from Athena, perhaps. We both ignored it.

* * * * * * *

(The old man continued his tale.)
On the way back to Athens, Diomedes went on talking, but he let me doze off. He was talking to himself, explicating, reasoning, making excuses, rehearsing what he would say to Theseus, and, I think, to Pluto himself when he met him face to face and fought for the life of Palamon.

My master's manner was certainly changed. Where, before, he had been almost joyous that I had somehow provided the vital clue he needed—and the affair was still a muddle, as if I possessed the one tile that completed a mosaic, and I couldn't see what the picture was—now he was grim, his actions urgent.

He told me that Palamon was haunted unto death, by a spirit who came to him in his dreams, and whispered a secret so painful that nothing could make him tell it, even to his physician to save his life, or to Emilia his wife because she loved him (for so, incredibly, it seemed she did, smitten was she like all the rest by this plague of love).

Now, explained Diomedes, the cause of the malady was clear. The gaoler's daughter was mad again, or never cured. She had murdered her rightful husband as we had seen and gone rampaging after Palamon. To what end? To love him or to slay him?

But why had she been dressed as for the grave when I saw her on the road in the night?

Because she had so dressed herself, in her madness, explained Diomedes, and then, somehow, probably by her own hand, she had died, and it was her ghost I saw, and her ghost which haunted Palamon unto death, and now, at last it all made sense—

Only it didn't make sense. I was too weary to say more than "What if she's not—?" and I couldn't finish the thought, and I felt down in my weariness, my face in Diomedes's lap, and he held onto me, as a father holds his son, to prevent me from falling out of the carriage, and I flattered myself to think that he held me with genuine affection.

I dreamed I was locked in a tomb with the gaoler's daughter. She chased me around and round, her grave-wrappings streaming, as she screamed in agony of the beauties of love.

"What if she's not?" I said again, half awake.

My master was too distracted to ask, "Not what?"

* * * * * * *

I awoke toward evening. We were in the vicinity of Athens, on the grounds of a great estate. What followed was an interview with the illustrious Palamon. It was the only time I ever beheld that noble man. I do not jest or exaggerate. He was a noble man. Such as character is visible in the lines of a face, or in the way a man carries his body, Palamon was, on first sight, clearly a man of heroic cast; but he was also a haunted one, haggard and hollow, like a mighty fortress now falling into ruin, the bold lines of its battlements still obvious to all, but everything within crumbling to pieces.

We sat in his garden and the evening drew on. Bats and night birds flittered overhead. I sat a little apart from the two men, a table in my lap, pretending to take notes, as a learned physician's assistant properly should.

"Only when I am alone does the phantom come to me," said

Palamon. "Whether I am asleep or awake, it comes. Somehow no one else ever sees it. But it comes, to whisper its horrible secret again and again—ask not, good Diomedes; you know it is a secret I must take to the grave with me to gild the tatters of my honor, and give the impression that I died a whole man. If others are with me and it does not come, still I am haunted by the knowledge that it is out there, that it can never rest because of what it has told me."

"I think I can lay it to rest," said Diomedes.

"I can only hope," said Palamon, "though I am without hope."

"But tell me the secret, and I can lay that to rest too."

"I would fall on my sword first."

Realizing there was no purpose in continuing such talk, my master turned to conversation to other matters, to pleasantries, to heroic tales of war, to the various other deeds Palamon and his dead brother Arcite had done, many of which had not been anywhere recorded or celebrated. I took careful notes then, fascinated, thinking this either material for some grand romance, or a treatise on madness.

Thus we filled the time. Hours past. It was fully night. Now, quickly, my master made a sacrifice to Hekate, goddess of witches, darkness, and of graves; and another to Athena, for protection, and yet a third to Diana for purity.

I shivered a little, not from cold, as the two of us drew off a distance and hid behind some bushes, while Palamon rested on his couch. My master held a lantern, carefully covered, so no light could escape.

We did not have long to wait. I saw something white moving between some trees, near the wall of the estate.

"Master!" I whispered.

"Hush! Silence! The spirit comes!"

The spirit came, hideous in its aspect, though in the form of a maiden; trailing smoke, seeming to smolder from within; its bones rattled as it came, and it held aloft a skull, which glowed like a lantern.

The spirit circled Palamon's couch, once, twice, thrice. I

could smell the fumes of its burning, like tar.

And the spirit spoke, saying, "Palamon, Palamon, I have come again from your brother Arcite to reproach you and to say that you are not an honorable man, who have stolen what you could not win—"

Then Diomedes stood up and shouted, "Spirit! Speak not!" He uncovered his lantern, filling the yard with light.

The spirit turned, astonished as any living miscreant would be, and it backed away a little bit as Diomedes and I approached. My master held up his hands. He began the rite of exorcism, commanding the spirit into silence, but instead it began to sing in a high, sweet voice. Its words were complete nonsense:

> *She is dead and gone, my lord,*
> *She is dead and gone.*
> *Let grow the apple and the grape,*
> *But pluck the bitter pear.*

"Spirit! I command you to be silent!"

"But I am a mad spirit, My Lord, and cannot be silent."

That was when I was certain. I saw, by the light of the lantern, that the apparition's legs were bruised. Her bare feet were bleeding, as I imagined they might be from climbing the stone wall that surrounded the garden.

I repeated my own enigmatic utterance from before.

"Master! What if she's not?"

"Not what boy? Not what?"

For an instant Diomedes was furious, but before he had time to react further I had flung myself onto the supposed ghost and wrestled it to the ground. It was solid enough. It wriggled in my grasp. I burned myself from the coals embedded in its clothing, but I didn't let go.

In an instant Palamon had lighted another lantern, and he and Diomedes stood over the fallen ghost, and all was revealed.

I held the gaoler's daughter in my arms. Still she fought. I couldn't get my hand over her mouth to silence her in time, and thus she was able to cry out for all to hear (and at the commotion some others of the household leaned out of windows and heard).

"Palamon! False lover! I loved you with all my heart. I risked everything for you! You spurned me! You cast me aside like an old shoe! Therefore I tell you again, Palamon, that Arcite did not die by any accident! I know how it was done. Someone, some agent of yours, maybe, someone who loved you and would do anything for you, slipped the poison into his drink before the battle. But he was too strong. The poison took too long to act. Then he defeated you, because he was the better man, but then he grew wobbly in the saddle afterwards, and fell and broke his head. You are not the victor! You are not the hero! No god has granted you any reprieve! You are a love's thief!"

"And you, poor girl," said Palamon slowly, "are love's assassin. I do not blame you. I blame love, who has slain all these good people."

I thought I heard something else just then, faint and far-away, a deep-voiced bell, tolling.

* * * * * * *

The rest is too appalling to tell in much detail. What I finally did say, once I had the girl firmly in my grasp was, "Master! I meant to say, *what if she is not dead?*"

Indeed she was not dead. Her shroud and bones were all mummery. She had soaked the shroud in a resin which retarded the coals, giving the effect of slow smoldering. There was a candle inside the skull.

Diomedes shook his head. "For once, good Phraates, you have missed the mark. You should have asked, *what if she is not mad?* She is not mad. She never was. Driven by passions and impossible longings, yes, but never deprived of her reason. Therefore I could not cure her. With her trailing flowers and mad songs, she was so conspicuous. But she could put off such things, and change her aspect, and move about all but invisibly, and seem just another drab. I don't doubt that she poisoned

Arcite, mingling with the servants unnoticed."

The girl hissed and snarled like an any cat. I held her tightly. Then she wept. Then she began to sing again.

"Master," I said, "I think it possible that she has *become* mad, now that it's all over."

Diomedes sighed. "If so, then we must cure her."

I hadn't noticed that Palamon had slipped away. Now there was a scream from within the house. I saw then, that he was gone. A woman came out into the garden, sobbing, telling us that Lord Palamon had fallen on his sword, and was dead.

The girl in my arms sang a slow, sad song in praise of Love.

* * * * * * *

We didn't get to cure the girl. Lord Theseus had her walled up, and therefore, as in my dream, she was buried alive and left to scream.

The Duke sat in judgment before Diomedes and myself. Hippolyta was there, and Emilia, shrouded in mourning.

"I cannot bring myself to believe," said Theseus, "that the Lord Palamon could have been in any way a party to this murder. He was a man of true honor."

"Nor do I believe it, dread Lord," said Diomedes. "It was the girl alone."

"Nevertheless, for fear of scandal, Palamon took his own life."

"It was an honorable thing, if regrettable."

"And his memory must remain honored. No suspicion of any taint must ever be voiced. You, physician, have performed your duties as best you can, and you shall be paid for them. You are a citizen of repute, and I trust your silence. But I think that, for caution's sake, we ought to have your slave killed. He knows too much. Fear not, I shall add an extra sum to your fee to cover the expense."

At that moment, all time seemed to stop. I felt only abject, helpless dread. I looked at my master, searching his face for some sign of humanity, some indication that I was more than a *thing* to be cast aside when I was no longer useful. Certainly I trembled. Maybe I even began to weep. It was useless to say anything, so I remained silent.

Diomedes looked to me. I could see him weighing the various factors in his mind. Then he turned to Theseus.

I tell you I thought nothing of love then, but I heard Pluto's bell quite clearly.

"You are mistaken, Lord," Diomedes said. He put his arm around me and drew me to him. "This is not a slave. This is Phraates, my assistant and my apprentice and my adopted son."

And still I heard it.

* * * * * * *

Old Phraates let out a rude noise, half a grunt, half a snore. His cup rolled about in his lap, staining his robe. Then he shook his head and seemed to come back to himself.

"Well? What do you think of that? I've told no one this story until now, until everybody else in it is safely dead these many years. So why do you think I told it to you, huh?"

I was amazed, but, as I have said, full of myself, and I proceeded to explicate the old man's tale, arranging the parts neatly for moral edification, showing how each god intervened in the lives of the characters: here Ares, in the war; Aphrodite in the intrigues of love; Artemis for the purity of that love; Zeus, bored and bemused, who moves all men about like game pieces on a board. By all of them, arbitrarily, are our lives governed. I went on at some length in this vein, until the old man spat angrily and hurled his cup against the hearth.

"Shut up! Shut up! Listen! I told you the story because it means nothing. I could have told it to a doorknob and it wouldn't have made any difference. Life and love and politics and wars, all mean nothing. That was what I learned, from that adventure, and over the years. All of us hear death's bell, when it is time, and we may have our comforts and our friendships before then,

but in the end nothing else matters. My master Diomedes was a good man, but a fool. He thought it was love. No, it was the echo of death, so powerful that Arcite heard it, then the gaoler's daughter, then Palamon. It resonates still. Hark! Listen! Listen!"

He held up his hand. I listened. There was only silence in the hall, but for the occasional snapping of the embers.

It was only after a long time, by the glassiness of his eye, that I could tell that the old man had died, right there, frozen in that position.

Before I went to summon Chosroes, I swept up the pieces of the broken cup. I noticed that, though it was cheap ware for casual use, there had been a design painted on it, that of two warriors locked in battle while a lady looked on. But now the picture was just a pile of fragments and could never be put back together.

That was my pretty allegory. Thus I explicated.

THE ADVENTURE OF THE DEATH-FETCH

In retrospect, the most amazing thing is that Watson confided the story to me at all. I was nobody, a nineteen-year-old college student from America visiting English relatives during Christmas break. I just happened to be in the house when the old doctor came to call. He had been a friend of my grandfather long before I was born, and was still on the closest terms with my several aunts; and of course he was *the* Doctor John Watson, who could have commanded the immediate and rapt attention of any audience he chose.

So, why did he tell me and only me? Why not, at least, my aunts? I think it was precisely because I was no one of any consequence or particular credibility and would soon be returning to school far away. He was like the servant of King Midas in the fairy tale, who can no longer bear the secret that the king has ass's ears. He has to "get it off his chest," as we Americans say. The point is not being believed, or recording the truth, but release from the sheer act of telling. The luckless courtier, fearing for his life, finally has to dig a hole in the swamp, stick his head in it, and whisper the secret. Not that it did him much good, for the wind in the rattling reeds endlessly repeated what he had said.

There being no swamp conveniently at hand for Dr. Watson, I would have to do.

The old gentleman must have been nearly eighty at the time. I remember him as stout, but not quite obese, nearly bald, with a generous white moustache. He often sat smoking by the remains of our fire long after the rest of the household had gone to bed. I imagined that he was reminiscing over a lifetime of wonderful adventures. Well, maybe.

I was up late too, that particular night, on my way into the kitchen for some tea after struggling with a wretched attempt at a novel. I chanced through the parlor. Doctor Watson stirred slightly where he sat.

"Oh, Doctor. I'm sorry. I didn't know you were still there." He waved me to the empty chair opposite him. I sat without a further word, completely in awe of the great man.

I swallowed hard and stared at the floor for perhaps five minutes, jerking my head up once, startled, when the burnt log in the fireplace settled, throwing off sparks. I could hear occasional automobiles passing by in the street outside.

Dr. Watson's pipe had gone out and he set it aside. He folded his age-spotted hands in his lap, cleared his throat, and leaned forward. He had my absolute attention. I knew that he was about to *tell a story*. My heart almost stopped.

"I am sure you know there were some cases of Sherlock Holmes which never worked out, and thus went unrecorded."

I lost what little composure I had and blurted, "Yes, yes, Doctor. You mention them from time to time. Like the one about the man and the umbrella—"

He raised a hand to silence me. "Not like that, boy. Some I never found the time to write up, and I inserted those allusions as reminders to myself; but others were *deliberately suppressed,* and never committed to paper at all, because Holmes expressly forbade it. One in particular—"

At least I didn't say anything as stupid as, *"Then why are you telling me?"* No, I had the good sense to sit absolutely motionless and silent, and just listen.

* * * * * * *

It was about this same season [*Watson began*] in the year

1900, a few days after Christmas if I recall correctly—I cannot be certain of such facts without my notebooks, and in any case the incident of which I speak was never entered into them—but I am certain it was a bright and brisk winter day, with new-fallen snow on the sidewalks, but no sense of festivity in the air. Instead, the city seemed to have reached a profound calm, a time to rest and tidy up and go on with one's regular business.

Holmes remarked how somehow, in defiance of all logic, it appeared that the calendar revealed patterns of criminality.

"Possibly the superstitions are true," I mused, "and lunatics really *are* driven by the moon."

"There may be scattered facts buried in the morass of superstition, Watson," said he, "if only science has the patience to ferret them out—"

We had now come, conversing as we walked, to the corner of Baker Street and Marylebone Road, having been abroad on some business or other—damn that I don't have my notes with me—when this train of thought was suddenly interrupted by an attractive, well-dressed young woman who rushed up and grasped Holmes by the arm.

"Mr. Sherlock Holmes? You *are* Mr. Sherlock Holmes, are you not?" Holmes gently eased her hand off him. "I am indeed, Miss—"

"Oh! Thank God! My father said that no one else could possibly save him!"

To my amazement and considerable irritation, Holmes began walking briskly, leaving the poor girl to trail after us like a common beggar. I'd often had words with him in private about these lapses of the expected courtesy, but now I could only follow along, somewhat flustered. Meanwhile the young lady—whose age I would have guessed at a few years short of twenty—breathlessly related a completely disjointed tale about a mysterious curse, approaching danger, and quite a bit else I couldn't make head or tail out of.

At the doorstep of 221B, Holmes turned on her sharply.

"And now Miss—I'm afraid I did not catch your name."

"Thurston. My name is Abigail Thurston."

"Any relation to Sir Humphrey Thurston, the noted explorer of Southeast Asia?"

"He is my father, as I've already told you—"

"I am not sure you've told me much of anything—yet!" Holmes turned to go inside. Miss Thurston's featured revealed a completely understandable admixture of disappointment, grief, and quite possibly—and I couldn't have blamed her—rage.

"Holmes!" I said. "Please!"

"And now Miss Abigail Thurston, as I have no other business this morning, I shall be glad to admit you." As she, then I, followed him up the stairs, he continued, "You must pardon my abrupt manner, but it has its uses."

When I had shown her to a chair and rung Mrs. Hudson for some tea, Holmes explained further, "My primary purpose has been to startle you into *sense,* Miss Thurston. A story told all in a jumble is like a brook plunging over a precipice—very pretty, but, alas, babbling. Now that the initial rush of excitement is past, perhaps now you can tell me, calmly and succinctly, why you have come to see me. I enjoin you to leave out none of the facts, however trivial they may seem to you. Describe the events *exactly,* in the order that they occurred, filling in such background as may be necessary to illuminate the entire tale."

She breathed deeply, then began in measured tones. "I am indeed the daughter of the explorer, Sir Humphrey Thurston. You are perhaps familiar with his discoveries of lost cities in the jungles of Indo-China. His books are intended for a limited, scholarly audience, but there have been numerous articles about him in the popular magazines—"

"Suffice it to say that I am familiar with your father and his admirable contributions to science. Do go on."

"My mother died when I was quite small, Mr. Holmes, and my father spent so much time abroad that he was almost a stranger to me. I was raised by relatives, under the supervision of a series of governesses. All this while Father seemed more a guardian angel than a parent, someone always looking out for my welfare, concerned and benevolent, but invisible. Oh, there were letters and gifts in the post, but he remained *outside* my actual life. Each time he came, we had to become acquainted all over again. Such is the difference in a child's life between six and eight and twelve. *I* had changed profoundly, while he was always the same, brave, mysterious, inevitably sunburnt from long years in the jungles and deserts; home for a short time to rest, write his reports, and perhaps give a few lectures before setting forth again in the quest of knowledge. So things have continued. This past month he has returned again, after an absence of three years, to discover his little girl become a *woman,* and again a stranger. He has promised to remain this time until I am married and secure in a home of my own—"

"Then it should be a happy occasion for you," said Holmes, smiling to reassure her, the corners of his mouth twitching to betray impatience. The smile vanished. "But I perceive it is not. Please get to the point then. *Why* have you come rushing to Baker Street on a winter's day when you would surely be much more comfortable in a warm house in the company of your much-travelled sire?"

She paused, looking alarmed once more, glancing to me first as if for reassurance. I could only smile and nod, wordlessly bidding her to continue.

"The first few days of his visit were indeed happy, Mr. Holmes, but very suddenly, a shadow came over him. For a week and more, he seemed distracted and brooding. Then five days ago he withdrew into his study, refusing to venture out for any reason. He is afraid, deathly afraid!"

"Of what, pray tell?"

"I cannot discern the central fear, exactly, only its broader effects. Certainly he has become morbidly afraid of his own reflection. He will not allow a mirror to be brought anywhere near him. He even shaves with his eyes closed, by touch alone, rather than risk seeing himself."

"This *is* extraordinary," I said.

"But surely," said Holmes, "this sort of mania is more in

Doctor Watson's line than mine, work for a medical man of a specialized sort, not a detective."

"Oh no, Sir! My father is completely sane. I am certain of that. But I am equally certain that he is not telling me everything, perhaps in an attempt to spare me some horror—for it must be a horror that makes so bold an adventurer cringe behind a locked door with a loaded elephant gun across his knees!"

I leaned forward and spoke to her in my most soothing medical manner. "I am sure, Miss Thurston, that your father has a very good reason for acting as he does, and that, indeed, his chief object is to protect you."

"Yes," said Holmes. "I am certain it is."

"His very words were, 'Summon Sherlock Holmes, girl, or I shall not live out the week!' So here I am. Please come and see him, Mr. Holmes, *at once!*"

Holmes shot to his feet. "Watson! How foolish of us to have even removed our hats and coats. Come!" He took our guest by the hand and helped her up. "As I said, Miss Thurston, I have no other business this morning."

* * * * * * *

It was but a short cab ride to the Thurston residence, in the most fashionable part of west London. We rode in silence, crowded together, the girl in the middle, Holmes deep in thought. Unconsciously almost, Miss Thurston took my hand for reassurance. I held her firmly, but gently.

It was admittedly an intriguing problem: what, if not a sudden mania, could cause so brave a man as Sir Humphrey Thurston to be paralyzed with fear at the sight of his own reflection?

As we neared the house, the girl suddenly struggled to stand up in the still moving cab.

"Father!"

She pointed. I had only a glimpse of a tall, muscular man on the further streetcorner, and noted the tan coat and top hat, white gloves, and silver-tipped stick. He turned at the sound of

Miss Thurston's cry, revealing a grey-bearded face, dark eyes, and a broad, high forehead, then moved speedily away in long strides, not quite running. Abruptly, he vanished down a side street.

Holmes pounded on the ceiling of the cab for the driver to stop and we three scrambled out, I attending to Miss Thurston and the driver while Holmes set off at a furious run, only to return moments later, breathing hard, having lost all trace of Sir Humphrey.

"I don't know what explanation I can offer," said Miss Thurston. "Perhaps my father's difficulty, mania or whatever it is, has passed, and I have wasted your time."

Holmes nodded to me.

"Mental disease is not my specialty." I said, "but from what medical papers I've read, and from the talk of my colleagues, I do not think it likely that so powerful a delusion would go away so quickly. It makes no sense."

"Indeed, it does not," said Holmes. "One moment, the man behaves as if he is faced with mortal danger. The next, he is out for a stroll as if nothing had happened, but he flees the approach of his beloved daughter and vanishes with, I must confess, remarkable speed and agility."

"What do we do now, Mr. Holmes?"

"If you would admit us to his chamber. Perhaps he left some clue."

"Yes, yes. I should have thought of that. Pray forgive me—"

"Do not trouble yourself, Miss Thurston. Only lead the way."

She unlocked the door herself. Although it was a fine, large house, there were no servants in evidence. I helped her off with her coat and hung it for her in a closet off to one side. As we ascended the front stairs, she hastily explained that another of her father's inexplicable behaviors was to give leave to the entire staff until—she supposed—the crisis had passed.

"Oh, I do fear that it *is* a mania, Mr. Holmes."

I was beginning to fear as much myself, but had scarcely a moment to consider the possibility when a voice thundered from above, "Abigail! Is that you?"

Miss Thurston looked to Holmes, then to me with an expression of utmost bewilderment and fright. I think she all but fainted at that moment. I made ready to catch her lest she tumble back down the stairs. Again came the voice, from somewhere off to the left of the top of the stairs. "Abigail! If that's you, speak up girl! If it's Hawkins, you damned blackguard, I have my gun ready and am fully prepared to shoot!" Holmes shouted in reply, "Sir Humphrey, it is Sherlock Holmes and his colleague Dr. Watson. We have been admitted by your daughter, who is here with us."

"Abigail?"

"Yes, Father, it is I. I've brought them as you asked."

Heavy footsteps crossed the floor upstairs. A door opened with a click of the lock being undone.

"Thank God, then..."

Holmes, Miss Thurston, and I were admitted into Sir Humphrey's study. I was astounded to confront the *same man* we had seen on the street. The broad shoulders, bearded face, high forehead, dark eyes, and athletic gait were unmistakable. But now he wasn't dressed for the outdoors. He wore a dressing gown and slippers. An elephant gun lay across the chair where he had obviously been sitting moments before. On the table by his right hand were a bottle and glass of brandy, a notebook, a pen and an uncapped ink jar.

"Thank God you are here, Mr. Holmes," he said. "Doubtless my daughter has told you of my distress and seeming madness. If anyone on Earth may convince me that I am *not* mad, it is you, Mr. Holmes. I can trust no one else to uncover the fiendish devices by which I have been made to see the impossible."

We all sat. Thurston offered Holmes and me glasses of brandy. Holmes waved his aside. I accepted out of politeness, but after a single sip placed it on the table beside me.

Sir Humphrey seemed about ready to speak, when Holmes interrupted.

"First, a question. Have you been, for any reason, outside of the house this morning?"

Thurston looked startled. "Certainly not. I have not been out of this *room* for five days—" He paused, as if uncertain of how to proceed.

It was Holmes's turn to be astonished, but only I, who knew him well, could detect the subtle change in his manner and expression. To the others he must have seemed, as before, calm and attentive, purely analytical.

The silence went on for a minute or two. Now I that had a chance to examine our surroundings, the room proved to be exactly what I expected, a cluttered assembly of mementoes and books, a large bronze Buddha seated on a teakwood stand, strangely demonic Asian masks hanging on the walls amid framed citations and photographs. In a place of honor behind his writing desk hung a portrait of a beautiful woman whose features resembled those of Abigail Thurston but were somewhat older. This I took to be her mother.

"Do go on, Sir Humphrey," said Holmes, "and tell us what has taken place during these five days in which you have never once left this room."

"You'll probably think I am out of my mind, Mr. Holmes. Indeed, I think so myself, whenever I am unable to convince myself that I am beguiled by some devilish trickery. For the life of me, I cannot figure out how it is *done*."

"How what is done, Sir Humphrey?"

"Mr. Holmes, do you know what I mean when I say I have seen my *death fetch*?"

Abigail Thurston let out a cry, then covered her mouth with her hand.

Holmes seemed unperturbed. "In the superstitions of many races, a man who is about to die may encounter his spirit-likeness. The German term is *doppelgänger*, meaning double-walker. Certainly such an apparition is held to be a portent of the direst sort, and to be *touched* by this figure means instantaneous death. You haven't been touched by it then, have you, Sir Humphrey?"

Thurston's face reddened. "If you mean to mock me, Mr. Holmes, then my faith in you is misplaced."

"I do not mock. Nor do I deal in phantoms. My practice stands firmly flat-footed upon the ground. No ghosts need apply. Therefore I must agree with your conclusion, even before I have examined the evidence, that you are the victim of trickery of some kind. But first, describe to me what you *think* you have seen."

"*Myself,* Mr. Holmes. My daughter has surely mentioned my sudden aversion to mirrors."

"Don't we all see ourselves in mirrors?"

"I saw myself *twice.*"

"Twice?"

"Five mornings ago, I stood before the mirror shaving, when a second image appeared in the glass, as if an *exact duplicate of myself* were looking over my shoulder. I whirled about, razor in hand, and confronted *myself* as surely if I gazed into a second mirror, only the face of this *other* was contorted with the most venomous hatred, Mr. Holmes, the most absolute malevolence I have ever beheld. The lips were about to form an utterance which I somehow *knew* would mean my immediate death.

"So I slashed frantically with my razor. I felt the blade pass through only the air, but the figure vanished, like a burst soap bubble."

"And it did not harm you in any way," said Holmes, "any more than a soap bubble—or some projected illusion of light and shadow."

"Oh no, Mr. Holmes, this was no magic-lantern show. It was a fully three-dimensional image. Each time I saw it, it was as real to my eyes as you and Dr. Watson appear now."

"You saw it, then, more than once?"

"Three times, Mr. Holmes, until I had the sense to remove all mirrors and reflective surfaces from the room. That is how it *gets in.* I am certain of that."

"And I am certain, Sir Humphrey, that *you* are certain of far more than you have told me. Unless you give me *all* of the facts,

112 | DARRELL SCHWEITZER

I cannot help you, however much your daughter may entreat me. Who, for instance, is the 'blackguard Hawkins' you took us for on the stairs?"

Thurston refilled his glass and took a long draught of brandy, then settled back. "Yes, you are right, of course, Mr. Holmes. I shall have to tell you and Dr. Watson everything." He turned to his daughter. "But you, my dear, perhaps should not hear what we have to say."

"Father, I think I am old enough."

"It is not a pretty story."

* * * * * * *

"My early years were wild," Sir Humphrey began. "I was no paragon of scientific respectability at twenty-one, but little more than a common criminal. I have never before admitted that I was dismissed from the Indian Army under extremely disreputable circumstances and only escaped court martial because a sympathetic officer allowed me time to flee, change my name, and disappear. The offense involved the pillage of a native temple, and the officer's sympathy had been purchased with some of the loot.

"And so, under another name, I wandered the East. I had no means by which to return to England, nor had I any desire to present myself to friends and family as a failure and a disgrace. Once in a very great while I dispatched a letter filled with fanciful, if artfully vague, tales of confidential adventures in government service.

"In the course of my travels I picked up several languages and a profound education in the ways of the world's wickedness. I fell in with the roughest possible company, and was myself more often than not on the wrong side of the law. In the gold fields of Australia there was a certain dispute and a man died of it, and once more I had to vanish. In Shanghai I worked as an agent for a wealthy mandarin, whose true activities, when they became known to the Chinese authorities, caused his head to be pickled in brine.

"But the blackest depths were in Rangoon, for there I met Wendall Hawkins. He was a vile rogue, Mr. Holmes, even among such company as I found him. Murderer, thief, pirate, and more—I am sure. He was a huge, powerful man with an enormous, dark beard, who used to jokingly boast—though I think he half believed it—that he was the reincarnation of Edward Teach, the notorious buccaneer commonly known as Blackbeard.

"Reckless as I was, my normal instinct would have been to avoid such a man as I would a live cobra, but he had something which fascinated me: an idol six inches in height, of a hideous, bat-winged dog, carven of the finest milky green jade, stylized in a manner which resembled the Chinese but wasn't. Its eyes were purest sapphires.

"Mr. Holmes, I was more than just a thieving lout in those days. Already the direction of my life's work was clear to me—though I had yet to learn its manner—for if ever I suffered from a true mania, it was the craving to penetrate the deepest secrets of the mysterious Orient. Oh, I wanted riches, yes, but more than that I hoped to come back to England famous, like some Burton or Livingston or Speke, having brought the light of European science to the darkest and most forbidden corners of the globe.

"I knew what this idol was, even before Wendall Hawkins told me. It was an artifact of the Chan-Tzo people who inhabit the Plateau of Leng in central Asia, in that unmapped and unexplored region northwest of Tibet, where theoretically the Chinese and Russian empires adjoin, but in fact no civilized person has ever set foot—for all the ravings of Madame Blavatsky contain much nonsense about the place. The very name, Chan-Tzo, is often mistranslated as 'Corpse-Eaters,' and so occultists whisper fearfully of the hideous rites of the 'Corpse Eating Cult of Leng.' In truth necrophagy is the least of Leng's horrors. The Chan-Tzo are 'Vomiters of Souls'...but I am far ahead of myself. Hawkins had the idol and he had a map—which had been acquired, he darkly hinted, at the cost of several lives—written in an obscure Burmese dialect. He needed me to translate. That was why he had come to me. Otherwise he would share his treasure-hunt with as few as possible—for that was what it was to be. We would journey to Leng armed to the teeth, slaughter any natives who stood in our way, and return to civilization rich men. I tried to console my conscience with the belief that I, at least, would be travelling as much for knowledge as for wealth, and that through my efforts this find could be of scientific value.

"Hawkins and ten others had pooled funds to buy a steam launch, which we christened, to suit our leader's fancy, the *Queen Anne's Revenge.* Once we had secured sufficient ammunition and supplies, we slipped up the Irriwaddy by night and journeyed deep into the interior, beyond the reach of any colonial authorities, ultimately anchoring at Putao near the Chinese border and continuing overland.

"I don't have to tell you that the trip was a disaster. Supplies went bad or disappeared. We all had fevers. What native guides we could hire or seize at gunpoint misled us, then got away. I alone could read the damned map, but it was cryptic, even if you could make out the script. Much of the time I merely guessed and tried to find our way by the stars.

"Many times I was certain that none of us would get back alive. The first to die was the crazy American, something-or-other Jones, a lunatic who carried a bullwhip and fancied himself an archaeologist. We found Jones in his tent, bloated to half again normal size, his face eaten away by foot-long jungle leeches.

"One by one the others perished, from accidents, from disease that might have been poisoning. Gutzman, the South African, caught a dart in the neck one night. Van Eysen, the Dutchman, tried to make off with most of our remaining food and clean water. Hawkins shot him in the back, then killed the Malay when he protested, and the Lascar on general principles. Another Englishman, Gunn, got his throat cut merely so that there would be one mouth less to feed.

"Since I alone could read the map—or pretended to—I was certain Hawkins needed me alive. In the end, there were only the two of us, ragged and emaciated wretches staggering on in a timeless delirium of pain and dread. It was nothing less than a living death.

"At last we emerged from the jungle and climbed onto the windswept tableland of central Asia. Still the journey seemed endless. I had no idea of where we were going anymore, for all I made a show of consulting the map over and over so that Hawkins would not kill me. Each night I dreamed of the black and forbidding Plateau of Leng, which was revealed to me in a series of visions, its ruins and artificial caverns of shocking antiquity, perhaps older even than mankind itself, as were the immemorial blasphemies of the Chan-Tzo.

"What Hawkins dreamed, I cannot say. His speech had ceased to be coherent, except on the point of threatening me should I waver from our purpose. I knew he was insane then, and that I would die with him, likewise insane, unless I could somehow escape his company.

"I was past thinking clearly. How fortunate, then, that my plan was simplicity itself—almost the bare truth rather than some contrived stratagem.

"I fell to the ground and refused to rise, no matter how much Hawkins screamed that he would blow my brains out with his pistol. I said I was dying, that his pistol would be a mercy. *He* would offer me no mercy. I was counting on that. Instead, he forced me to translate the map for him and make notes as best I could. There was nothing to write with by a thorn and my own blood, but I wrote, and when he was satisfied, he laughed, folded the map into his pocket, took *all* our remaining supplies, and left me to my fate on the trackless, endless plain.

"And so we parted. I hoped I had sent him to Hell, deliberately mixing up the directions so he'd end up only the Devil knew where. He, of course, assumed I would be vulture's meat before another day or two. "But I did not die. Mad with fever and privation, my mind filled with fantastic and horrible hallucinations, I wandered for what might have been days or even weeks, until, by the kindness of providence alone, I stumbled into the camp of some nomads, who, seeing that I was a white man, bore me on camel-back into the Chinese province of Sinkiang and there turned me over to a trader, who brought me to a missionary. "This proved to be my salvation, both physical and otherwise. I married the missionary's daughter, Abigail's mother, and largely through the influence of her family I later found a place on a much more respectable Anglo-French expedition to Angkor. That was the true beginning of my scientific career. Still the mysteries of the East haunted me, but my cravings were directed into proper channels until I achieved the renown I have today."

* * * * * * *

At this point Sir Humphrey paused. The only sound was the slow ticking of a great clock in some other room. Abigail Thurston's face was white from the shock of what she had heard. She scarcely seemed to breathe. Holmes sat very still, his chin held in his hand, staring into space.

I was the one who broke the silence.

"Surely, Sir Humphrey, there is more to the story than that. I don't see how your luckless expedition or whatever fate the rascal Hawkins must have met has anything to do with the here and now." Thurston's reaction was explosive.

"Damn it, man! It has *everything* to do with my predicament and what may well be my inevitable fate. But...you are right. There is more to tell. After many years of roving the world, giving lectures, publishing books, after I was knighted by the Queen—after my past life seemed a bad dream from which I had finally awakened—I thought I was safe. But it was not to be. *This past fortnight I began to receive communications from the fiend Hawkins!*"

"Communications?" said Holmes. "How so?"

"There. On the desk."

Holmes reached over and opened an ornately carven, lacquered box, removing a sheaf of papers. He glanced at them briefly and gave them to me.

"What do you make of them, Watson?"

"I cannot read the writing. The paper is an Oriental rice-paper. The penmanship shows the author to be under considerable mental strain, perhaps intoxicated. Notice the frequent scratchings and blottings. Beyond that, I can make out nothing."

Sir Humphrey spoke. "The language is an archaic—some would say degenerate—form of Burmese, the script a kind of code used by criminals in the Far East. Between these two elements, I am perhaps the only *living* man who can read what is written here, for Wendall Hawkins *is not alive*, if his words are to be believed."

"Surely if he is dead," said Holmes, "your troubles are at an end."

"No, Mr. Holmes, they are not, for all of these letters were written *after* Hawkins's death—long after it. It seems that he *reached* the Plateau of Leng, which I saw only in visions. There the almost sub-human priests of the Chan-Tzo murdered him after what might have been *years* of indescribable tortures, then brought him back into a kind of half-life as an animate corpse at their command, hideously disfigured, the skin flayed from his face, his heart ripped out, the cavity in his chest filled with inextinguishable fire. He is in implacable now, driven both by the will of his masters and his own rage for revenge against me, whom he blames for his unending agony. He knows all the secrets of the Chan-Tzo priests, and the conjuring of death-fetches is easily within his power."

"He says all *that* in these letters?" I asked.

"That and more, Dr. Watson, and if it is true, I am defenseless. My only hope is that Mr. Holmes and yourself can prove me to be *deluded,* the victim of a *hoax* perpetrated by the vile Hawkins who has no doubt returned, but returned, I still dare to hope, as no more than a mortal villain. If you can do this, I certainly have the means to reward you handsomely for your services."

"My services are charged on a fixed scale," said Holmes, "but let us not concern ourselves with the monetary details now. I shall indeed collar this Hawkins for you and unmask his devices—which I am sure would make the tricks of our English spirit mediums child's play in comparison—but they are devices none the less. For what else can they be?"

"Mr. Holmes, I will be forever in your debt."

"We shall watch and wait until Hawkins is forced to show his hand. But first, I think Dr. Watson should escort Miss Abigail to a safer place, my own rooms, which I shall not be needing until this affair is concluded." When Thurston's daughter made to protest, Holmes turned to her and said, "You have been a heroine, but now that the battle is actually joined, I think it best that you remove yourself from the field. Will you go with Dr. Watson?"

"Whatever you say, Mr. Holmes."

"Splendid. Now I must busy myself examining the house inside and out, to discover any way our enemy might use to gain entrance." Thurston picked up the elephant gun and lay it across his lap, then began idly polishing the barrel with a cloth.

"I've survived five days like this. I think I shall be safe here behind the locked door for a little while longer yet. Your plan makes excellent sense, Mr. Holmes."

We left Sir Humphrey alone in the room. As Holmes and I escorted Miss Thurston down the stairs, the detective asked me, "Well, Watson, what do you think?"

"A unique case, Holmes. One worthy of your talents."

"About Sir Humphrey. What about him?"

"I judge him to be of fundamentally sound mind, but what superstitious fears he may harbor are being played upon by the murderous Hawkins, who sounds himself to be completely mad."

"Mad or not, he shall have to manifest himself in a decidedly *material* form before long, at which point he will be susceptible to capture by mundane means."

"One thing doesn't fit, Holmes. Who, or what, did we see upon our arrival here? Sir Humphrey hadn't been out of the room."

"An impostor, possibly a trained actor in league with Hawkins. I agree that all the pieces of the puzzle are not yet in place. But have patience. You know my methods."

"I am so glad that you and Dr. Watson will help Father," Miss Thurston said softly as we reached the base of the stairs. "You are sent from Heaven, both of you."

Holmes smiled indulgently. "Not from nearly so far, but we shall do what we can."

Alas, we could do but little. As we stood there at the base of the stairs and I helped Miss Thurston on with her coat, she turned and chanced to look back up the stairs. Suddenly she screamed.

"Good God!" I exclaimed.

Near the top of the stairs was a figure who appeared to be Sir Humphrey, but dressed for the outside, in coat and top hat, as we had seen him before. He *could not* have gotten past us.

"You! Stop!" Holmes was already in pursuit, bounding up the steps three at a time.

The figure moved so swiftly the eye could hardly follow, and soft-footedly. I heard only Holmes's boots pounding on the wooden stairs. Then there came a cry from within the study. Sir Humphrey shouted something in a foreign language, his tone that of abject terror, his words broken off in a gurgling scream. The elephant gun went off with a thunderous roar.

I left Miss Thurston and hurried up after Holmes. By the time I reached the study door, which was blown apart from the inside as if a cannonball had gone through it, Holmes was inside.

He rushed out again, his eyes wild, his face bloodless, and he saw Miss Abigail Thurston coming up behind me.

"For the love of God, Watson! Don't let her in!"

"Father!" she screamed. "Oh, you must let me pass!"

For all she struggled, I held her fast.

"Watson! Do not let her through no matter what happens! It

is just...too horrible!"

I think that was the only time I ever saw Sherlock Holmes truly shocked, at a loss for words.

I forced Miss Thurston back down the stairs despite her vehement protests, holding onto her until the police arrived, which they did shortly, summoned by the neighbors who had heard the screams and the shot. Only after she had been conveyed away in a police wagon, accompanied by a patrolman, was I able to examine the body of Sir Humphrey Thurston, who was indeed murdered, as I had feared.

Though still seated in his chair, he had been mutilated hideously, almost beyond recognition.

His throat was cut from ear to ear. That was enough to have killed him. But the flesh had been almost entirely torn away from his face, and a strange series of symbols, like the ones I had seen in the letters, had been carved in the bare bone of his forehead. The crown of his skull had been smashed in by some blunt instrument, and—it revolted me to discover—most of his brain was gone. The final detail was the worst, for it had been deliberately designed to mock us. The still smoking elephant gun lay across his lap, and, carefully placed so that it would be *reflected in the mirrored surface of the polished gun barrel,* was a small jade idol with emerald eyes, a stylized figure of a bat-winged dog.

"Yes, Holmes," I said, "it is entirely too horrible."

* * * * * * *

Dr Watson stopped telling the story, and I, the nineteen-year-old American college student, could only gape at him open-mouthed, like some imbecile, trying not to reach the attractively obvious conclusion that the good doctor's mind had gone soft after so many years. It was a terrible thing, just to entertain such a notion. I almost wept.

I would have remained there forever, frozen where I sat, wordless, had not Dr. Watson gone on.

"It was a case which I could not record, which Holmes *ordered* me to suppress on pain of the dissolution of our friendship. It just didn't work out."

"Wh-what do you mean, didn't work out?"

"I mean exactly that. The affair concluded too quickly and ended in abject failure. We accomplished nothing. He would have no more of the matter, the specifics, as he acidly phrased it, being left to the 'official imagination,' which, sure enough, concluded the murder to be the work of a madman or madmen, perhaps directed by a sinister Oriental cult, a new Thuggee. But even the police could not account for the powerful stench of *decay* which lingered in the explorer's study even long after the body had been removed, as if something long dead had invaded, done its worst, and departed as inexplicably as it had come. "Enormous pressure was brought to bear to prevent any accurate reportage in the newspapers, to prevent panic. I think those instructions came from the very highest level. Sir Humphrey's obituary, ironically, listed the cause of his demise as an Asiatic fever. I signed the death certificate to that effect.

"My own conclusions were profoundly disturbing. The mystery could not be resolved. What we—even Miss Thurston—had witnessed were not merely unlikely, but *impossible*.

"'I *reject* the impossible,' said Holmes vehemently. 'as a matter of policy. Such things *cannot be*—'

"'You and I and the girl saw, Holmes. They *are*.'

"'No, Watson! No! The irrational has *no place* in detective work. We must confine ourselves to the tangible and physical, carefully building upon meticulous reason, or else the whole edifice of my life's work crumbles into dust. Against the supernatural, I am helpless, my methods of no use. My methods *have* been useful in the past, don't you think? And so they shall be in the future, but we must remain within certain bounds, and so preserve them.'"

* * * * * * *

Again I, the college boy, was left speechless.

"Holmes made me swear an oath—and I swore it—never to write up this case—and I never wrote it—"

Had he, in a sense at least, broken his oath by telling me? I dared not ask. Was there some urgency now, of which had lately become aware?

"I wanted to tell someone," was all he said. "I thought I should."

King Midas. Ass's ears. Who will believe the wind in the reeds? I merely know that a week after I returned to school in America I received a telegram saying that Dr. Watson had died peacefully of heart failure, sitting in that very chair by the fire. A week later a parcel arrived with a note from one of my aunts, expressing some bewilderment that he had wanted me to have the contents.

It was the idol of the bat-winged dog.

SHERLOCK HOLMES, DRAGON-SLAYER
(The Singular Adventures of the Grice Patersons in the Island of Uffa, as if Written by Lord Dunsany)

It was in the course of one of those long afternoons at our club when no billiards were played, that the subject of the conversation turned to romance. The members had gathered around the fireplace in comfortable chairs. The waiter moved quietly among us, serving drinks. Someone spoke of tragic lovers, of Tristan and Isolde, Lancelot and Guinevere, Aeneas and Dido, drawing out of these and other examples some lofty and sobering theme which, in the light of what followed, I understandably cannot recall. A boorish member, who really shouldn't have been in our club at all, began praising the works of a certain modern novelist known to the rest of us only by avoidance, an author of truly appalling sentimentality. Several hearers sighed or groaned. One tried to steer the conversation back out of the mire, but the Boorish Member failed to perceive any of these signals and continued his discourse.

There was only one thing for it. I hastily signalled the waiter and ordered a large whiskey and soda, not for myself, but for a certain other clubman present, who had as yet remained silent. This particular gentleman had been extraordinarily well-travelled in his younger days, and could always be relied upon, when suitably fueled by the very potation I had just ordered, to narrate some fascinating episode from his past adventures. He, if anyone, could rescue us from further droning paeans to popular literature.

The Clubman sipped his drink for a long while, and I almost feared that he had failed me, but of course he had not.

He cleared his throat suddenly, like a motor-car sputtering to life.

"I met Sherlock Holmes once," said he.

"What's *that* got to do with romance?" said the Boorish Member.

I don't think the rest of us cared if it did or not.

"It concerned one of his unrecorded cases, which Doctor Watson only mentioned in passing."

"Ah. Do go on." This last came from the Skeptic, a lawyer who, if truth must be told, remained forever jealous of our storytelling Clubman, and devoted much vain effort to proving him a liar. Now he regarded his foe expectantly, as a cobra does its victim.

"The good Doctor, as you know, never wrote up all the cases. There's a dispatch box in a vault at Charing Cross containing a treasure-trove of notes."

"Yes, yes," interrupted the Boorish Member. "I read something about one of them once. It was called 'Riccoletti and His Abominable Wife.' Probably some damned nonsense about an Italian nobleman married to a yeti." He actually slapped his thigh, to emphasize the hilarity of his own attempted witticism.

The rest of us looked away discreetly.

"The case in which I became involved," said the storytelling Clubman, "was the one Watson so intriguingly entitled 'The Singular Adventures of the Grice Patersons in the Island of Uffa.' It did indeed involve romance, and also, incidentally, a treasure-trove."

I saw that our storyteller was now gaining the momentum of his narrative, but his whiskey glass was perilously near to empty, so I ordered him another.

The Skeptic spoke. "Of course you have read the monograph by the Danish scholar Anderson on that very case."

"A brilliant piece of work, too," said the Clubman. "Inevitably, though, there are certain points in it which are incompletely expounded or even incorrect. Yet at times Anderson's speculations are almost uncanny in their accuracy, especially when you consider that Anderson was never there. I cannot claim to be his intellectual superior when I say that I must correct him on some of the details, for, you see, I have an unfair advantage. I *was* there, and witnessed nearly everything."

"Where precisely was *there?*" the Skeptic asked.

* * * * * * *

"You will appreciate why I cannot be too specific," said the Clubman. "There are certain things one must draw a veil over. Suffice it to say it was in the Fen Country, near Thetford, in those vast marshlands which attract so many sportsmen in the appropriate fishing and shooting seasons.

"This was not the appropriate season, however, but a windy night in late November, and I chanced to be crossing the halfway-frozen fens on business of my own. It was nearly nightfall, and my business was pressing. Imagine me, if you will, somewhat younger and more vigorous than I am today, bundled against the weather, my long scarf trailing as I leaned into the wind. I wore knee-boots for wading through the icy rivulets and carried an electric torch in my right hand. In my left, I held a firm, long stick, with which to prod the ground in front of me to test for quicksand.

"I was proceeding in such a fashion when suddenly I heard a woman scream.

"Of course I broke into a run, and had there been any quicksand in my path just then, I'm sure it would have claimed me. The lady cried out her distress once more, and then the beam of my torch caught her as she struggled with some adversary on the top of a low hill. She was young and, I could tell even under the circumstances, a striking beauty, though dressed almost mannishly in boots and mudstained trousers and a heavy coat, as if prepared for adventure. Well, she was having an adventure now. I think there was blood on her face, but she did not seem greatly injured. She put up a terrific fight against some opponent who was only a dark shape.

"I called out for him to unhand her, but as I did the two of them merely *vanished* into thin air, and her cries ceased.

"I thought then that I had seen a ghost, perhaps re-enacting some ancient horror. The Fen Country is notoriously haunted, you know, this particular district even more so than most. Before setting out, I had had my supper at a public house in the nearest village, and the local people filled my ears with such tales, while grumbling about rich Londoners who refused to 'leave alone what should be left alone.' Previously, I had considered such admonitions mere rustic superstition, but now I was less certain.

"I had not long to meditate upon this theme. I splashed through half-frozen mud and climbed the hill, which rose above the surrounding marshland like an enormous, beached whale. A hillock, really, but the only high ground for miles around.

"Suddenly someone tapped me on the shoulder with a stick and said, 'You there! What is the meaning of this?'

"I whirled about, and by the light of my torch beheld a face I had not seen in twenty years.

"'Good God! John Watson!' I exclaimed.

"'Do I know you, Sir?' he said, his manner still guarded.

"Watson and I had been chums in our youth, before he went off to medical school and the army. We had once belonged to a boys' secret society together. I swiftly transferred my torch to my left hand, then reached out and gave him the secret handshake.

"A broad smile broke across that redoubtable face. He laughed and embraced me warmly. 'So it *is* you, old friend!'

"I assured him that it was, and remarked on how I had admired his writings in *The Strand* and followed his career closely. But he was in no mood to chat, and this was hardly the place for it.

"'Holmes and I are involved in a most difficult investigation,' he said.

"'Perhaps I can be of some assistance?'

"'Perhaps you can. Yes, come along.'

"He swiftly led me along the long axis of the hill, then down the slope to one side, to where pale light flickered from what appeared to be a cave mouth. I paused, involuntarily calling to mind some of the local superstitions about goblins which assume pleasing shapes and lure travellers to their doom.

"Watson must have read my mind. He gave me the secret handshake right back, something no goblin could ever have done. There is a story behind that handshake and its efficacy against goblins, but I shall save it for another time.

"Watson hurried me along. 'We mustn't keep Holmes waiting.'

"So the two of us descended into the opening, which proved to be the tunnel-mouth of an archaeological excavation, shored up with planks. Picks, shovels, buckets, and sifting-screens lay about, somewhat untidily, suggesting that the workers had deserted their duties in some haste. Within, crouched around a small table and examining a chart by the light of storm lanterns, were two gentlemen, one unknown to me, the other unmistakably the world-famous detective, Mr. Sherlock Holmes.

"Since we were out in the wilderness and the weather was appropriate, Holmes was actually wearing his famous deerstalker, which, of course, numerous illustrations and stageplays to the contrary, he would never have worn in town any more than he would have worn the feathered head-dress of a Red Indian. But in the country, it was a most practical piece of head-gear. In fact, I was wearing one myself.

"'Since you have Watson's trust,' said he, 'I can take you into confidence and rely upon your discretion.'

"He introduced the other gentleman to me as Henry Grice Paterson, the son of a wealthy shipping magnate, lately turned amateur archaeologist.

"I told them what I had seen on my arrival.

"'Heaven help her!' Grice Paterson exclaimed before I had even finished. 'It is Beatrice, and she is in peril!' He leapt to his feet, but Holmes and Watson both caught hold of him.

"'Nothing will be gained by rushing madly into the darkness,' said the great detective, 'except perhaps your unfortunate death.'

"'But, my beloved wife—'

"'If you hurl yourself into the quicksand, what good will that do her? *Think,* man, before you act, and perhaps she may yet be rescued.'

"'We can't just loiter here while—'

"Now Holmes rose to his feet, stooping beneath the low earthen ceiling. 'You are absolutely correct. We must search at once. Every second is precious.'

"So the three of them took up lanterns. Holmes led the way. I followed, and as the beam of my torch played over the tunnel walls and floor, I couldn't help but notice the occasional bit of litter which looked for all the world like ancient, human bones.

"Outside, Watson and Grice Paterson shouted for Beatrice, while Holmes bade me shine my torch on the ground. He was looking for, I suppose, footprints. After a time, there was only silence, but for the lonely howling of the wind. We four stood beneath the brilliant stars, in such darkness and isolation that it was hard to imagine this to be other than primordial wilderness. London, or even a cosy pub in a nearby village, seemed fantastic memories, something out of another world.

"'I fear that I am unable to dismiss what we were told about this place,' said Grice Paterson at last. 'It *is* haunted.'

"'Surely you don't believe the stories of ghosts and monsters,' said Watson.

"'I don't know what to believe anymore,' moaned Grice Paterson. He turned to me imploringly. 'Into *thin air,* you said, Sir?'

"'So it appeared,' I had to admit.

"'So it *appeared,*' echoed Holmes sharply. 'That is the key to it. Things are seldom what they appear, and superstition runs wild with mere appearance, rather than calmly discovering the more subtle truth which may lie beneath that appearance.'

"'I take it that you don't believe in ghosts, Mr. Holmes,' I said.

"He snorted contemptuously. 'To me, the spooks need not apply. My methods admit no room for the supernatural.'

"It was hardly the time for me to relate that I had actually met several spooks already in the course of my travels and that there were perhaps more things in heaven and earth than dreamt of even in the philosophy of Sherlock Holmes. At leisure, such an argument might have proved stimulating, but now, of course, a lady was in danger and a mystery was to be solved. Also, it was bitterly cold there, in the wind and darkness, on top of that mound.

"'Watson,' said Holmes. 'Fetch the probing rods.'

"Watson scrambled back into the tunnel, then returned with several metal rods about a yard long and thick as a man's finger. They were bluntly pointed on one end. These, with effort, we drove into the half-frozen ground. As we worked, Holmes filled in much which I had already surmised, but he told the tale more vividly than I ever could, and so I must merely summarize.

"This place, this hillock to be precise, was known from ancient times as the Island of Uffa. Perhaps a thousand years ago the fens were even swampier than they are today, and it was a true island. Hither, in the most obscure period of our country's history, about A.D. 570, came a fierce Saxon chieftain, Uffa, to build a fortification from which he could control the surrounding countryside and dominate his equally barbaric rivals. But Uffa did not prosper. As the cowering British peasantry had warned him, the place was haunted. One by one his loyal thanes met hideous deaths, often found torn to pieces in the morning, even partially devoured. There was talk of the Dragon of Uffa, a huge beast which no surviving witness had ever seen. It was also called King Uffa's Bane, in the sagas. The slaughter continued, yet, with the grim and steadfast loyalty expected of a war-band in those days, Uffa's men remained with him. They set traps for the monster, attempted stratagems, fought, and diminished in number. The king sent for Beowulf, but Beowulf was occupied with a similar case in Scandinavia at the time.

"'You might call him the world's first consulting monster-slayer,' Holmes joked uncharacteristically, but, I believe, with the serious purpose of relieving tension and maintaining Grice Paterson's faltering morale.

"'Mr. Holmes,' said he. 'I fail to understand why you relish such details if, as you say, monster stories are irrelevant.'

"'Even things which are factually untrue may be quite relevant,' replied Holmes, 'particularly when they lead people to act on the basis of belief.'

"He resumed his account of Uffa's protracted doom. It could still be the subject of a stupendous romance, if written by someone more capable than a modern sentimental novelist. King Uffa had a beautiful queen, named Hrothwealda, who stayed by his side, magnificent to the end. On the last night of their lives, both of them took up spears, swords, and shields. Both wore gleaming armor, for Hrothwealda was a warrior queen, as formidable as her husband. When the dragon came for them, man and wife fought as comrades. But in vain. The dragon devoured Hrothwealda as an alligator gulps down a sheep.

"It must have seemed cruelly inexplicable that it spared King Uffa. But it did, merely towering over him, as he clung to his broken spear and mourned for Queen Hrothwealda.

"The dragon's mistress explained why. There emerged from the darkness a fantastic figure, such as only that barbaric age could have produced, a woman clad in skins and dangling necklaces of human bones, with bronze serpents coiled around her arms and the horns of some beast affixed to her head. This was the witch Graxgilda, who had lusted after King Uffa since girlhood and had now come to claim him. She hadn't cared about the thanes, though it was convenient to get them out of the way, loyal as they were to both Uffa and to Uffa's lady. It was that lady, Hrothwealda, whom the witch desired to destroy. Now that she had done so, she demanded that Uffa become her lover.

"Of course he did not. He fell on his sword, to join his beloved wife in death. Graxgilda raged afterward. She bade the dragon destroy the king's fort, which it easily did, and she left the creature in the vicinity to haunt the mound, and to guard Uffa's treasure until the end of time.

"'I must confess, Sir,' said Grice Paterson to me when Holmes had finished his account, 'that even as Schliemann regarded the tales of Homer as having some basis in fact, I did not think the story of King Uffa to be entirely a fable. I was, and still am, certain that such a Saxon marauder actually lived in this district, and that he and the fruits of his depredations lie buried in this mound. When I discovered the location of the mound, I began excavations at once, even in this inconvenient season, lest someone else arrive at the same conclusion, or the prevalence of sportsmen in the Spring give the secret away.

"'Our immediate problem,' said Holmes, 'is not so much that of preserving the secret, which has obviously already been compromised, or even of finding the king and his treasure. Instead we must concentrate on the discovery of the secret passageway into which Beatrice Grice Paterson has been carried, not by any ghostly Saxon warrior or even a dragon, but by a mundane kidnapper. I am sure the passage is quite near to this very spot, from which the lady seemed to *vanish into thin air,* as the estimable gentleman phrased it.'

"The great detective resumed his probing.

"'Mr. Holmes,' said Grice Paterson. 'Do you truly believe there is still hope for my Beatrice?'

"'Most certainly,' replied Holmes, 'if we work to our utmost to find that passage.' So we four labored, Holmes silent and intent, studying every clue, while Watson, slightly out of breath from the exertion, filled me in on the rest.

"'Mr. and Mrs. Grice Paterson began their diggings, despite the inclimate season and the objections of the local folk, whose numerous warnings could be taken as half-veiled threats. For a week or so, things went well. Some ancient Saxon weapons were found, badly rusted, of course, but of definite scientific value. Then came the bones at least a dozen human beings, almost as if, following a custom more barbaric than even those of the pagan Saxons, the king had been buried with all his retainers.'

"'The odd thing was,' interjected Grice Paterson as he drove his probe into the ground once more, 'that most of those bones were mutilated, broken to bits. The larger pieces had toothmarks on them, as if the ancient graves had been violated by some enormous scavenging animal.

"'But still there was nothing of monetary value,' said Watson, 'until Mrs. Grice Paterson found the jar of coins, the...what were they called?'

"'*Sceats.* Small, crude, Anglo-Saxon silver pieces, many of them bearing the monogram of King Uffa himself, thus establishing his historical existence once and for all. You cannot imagine how excited Beatrice and I were by this wonderful discovery, which was soon followed by the unearthing of what must have been the actual treasury of the ancient king—hundreds of gold pieces, many of them Byzantine, issued during the reign of Justinian the Great and his immediate successor, and worth, needless to say, a great deal on the open market, but still more valuable to science, since they demonstrated a level of commerce between early Anglo-Saxon England and the East hitherto unsuspected.'

"'Then things began to go terribly wrong,' said Watson.

"Grice Paterson grunted as he pulled his probe out of the ground. 'The hauntings began. Our workmen, who were not locals, of course, but brought in from more outlying districts at considerable expense, began to report disturbing sounds, which first I assured them were merely the wind blowing across the tunnel mouth as one blows across a bottle. But no, they insisted. These sounds came from beneath the ground. *Like 'owlin' and wailin' an' gnashin' o' big teeth!* as the foreman colorfully expressed it.'

"'It seemed that the legendary terrors which plagued King

Uffa had returned,' said Watson. His probe was stuck. I helped him draw it out.

"'But Mr. Holmes did not believe me,' said Grice Paterson, 'even after the first death.'

"'One of the workmen was murdered in the night while guarding the site,' said Watson. 'His fellows found him in the morning, horribly mutilated. I'm afraid the others showed little of the steadfast loyalty of King Uffa's thanes. They took to their heels, and two more failed to reach the village. They vanished in broad daylight. Holmes speculated that they fell into quicksand. Furthermore, such clues as a footprint that did not belong, cigar ashes found when the workmen all smoked pipes, and other such seeming trivia of the sort from which he so brilliantly draws his conclusions convinced Holmes that someone might be trying to frighten everyone off, and had resorted to murder to get at the treasure.'

"'I knew that only Mr. Holmes could help us,' said Grice Paterson, 'no matter what the cause, supernatural or otherwise. But, this very night, as we were examining our diagrams of the underground maze we have just begun to uncover, Beatrice stepped out for a breath of fresh air—the lantern smoke in so confined a place can become very close—and was carried off, as you saw, Sir, by some fiend or dragon or whatever—'

"Suddenly Holmes cried out. 'Watson! Come here! I've found it as I knew we would!'

"We all rushed to where he knelt down. He pushed his probe through the earth freely, drew it out, and pushed again with little effort, indicating a hollow space beneath. '"A secret passage, as I long suspected,' said Holmes. 'Now if we can but find the opening.'

"Grice Paterson, perhaps over-eager, plunged his own probing rod into the ground as hard as he could, as if he were driving a harpoon. He must have tripped something, because the earth instantly gave way beneath himself, Holmes, and Watson. The three of them tumbled into darkness, leaving me alone on the hilltop.

"I was startled half out of my wits, yes, and for an instant fancied the dragon must have swallowed all three, but then reason prevailed. I directed my torch beam down the hole that had opened up, and saw that my stalwart companions were unhurt and brushing themselves off. Holmes struck a match and relit one of the lanterns. By this light and that of my electric torch, numerous side passageways were revealed, part of an underground labyrinth.

"'You stay here and keep watch,' Holmes instructed me. 'We shall return shortly with the answer to the mystery.'

"And, like a heroic champion of old, he confidently led his troops into the darkness, and that was the last I saw of any of them until much later, after the affair had concluded."

* * * * * * *

At the point the Clubman paused and took a long sip of his whiskey, He leaned back in his chair and seemed almost ready to doze off.

"But—but—!" the Skeptic sputtered. "You can't end the story like that!"

"Oh, Holmes wrapped things up pretty neatly. At the center of the labyrinth was a chamber, to which the kidnapper had carried Beatrice Grice Paterson. She was unharmed, fortunately, but for a bruise or two and a nasty cut on her forehead, where the blackguard had assaulted her. He was an old business rival of Grice Paterson's father, who had fallen into bankruptcy more through his own incompetence than anything the elder Grice Paterson might have done. A chap named Ponderby—"

"Haw! I bet he was ponderous enough!" The Boorish Member slapped his thigh again, guffawing loudly at his unwelcome attempt at humor. He slurped his drink *inexcusably* and the waiter gently but firmly took the rest of it away from him. A moment later he was merely snoring, to the immense relief of all others present. (I am pleased to report that this fellow is no longer a member of our club, but has since transferred his allegiance to the Drones.)

Our storyteller patiently waited until the distraction was past.

"In fact, Ponderby was dead, hideously mangled, as if mauled by a tiger. Mrs. Grice Paterson sobbed something about a huge claw that came at him out of the darkness. Watson told me all about it later. It was his diagnosis, and Holmes and Grice Paterson concurred, that the lady was hysterical and perhaps hallucinating, due to the blow on the head.

"That was the end of the adventure, then. The rest of the artifacts excavated from that mound were turned over to the proper authorities. The mystery was solved, although not as neatly as Holmes might have liked. Even he could not satisfactorily account for Ponderby's death. Therefore he did not allow Watson to publish any account of the Singular Adventures of the Grice Patersons in the Island of Uffa."

* * * * * * *

Now the Clubman sat back, as if daring his adversary the Skeptic to bait him further. He finished his whiskey, and, without being told, the waiter brought him another. All was silent in that room but for the Boorish Member's rhythmic snoring.

"It's utterly preposterous," the Skeptic ventured at last. "This rot about King Uffa and a dragon—"

"You can read about it in the *Anglo-Saxon Chronicle*."

"Not in any version I've read."

"It's not in the official version, certainly not the one published by Everyman's Library for the common reader."

Someone snickered. The Clubman and the Skeptic regarded one another politely enough, but beneath the surface of mere appearance, they were two scorpions in a jar, duelling to the death.

"It's still not much of an ending," said the Skeptic weakly. "Just a fairy-story, really."

"I never said it *was* the ending, now, did I?"

* * * * * * *

The Clubman sipped his whiskey and resumed his tale.

"Everything I have told you, even about events in the remote past, is unquestionably true. I have *those* facts on the best authority."

"And what authority might that be?" demanded the Skeptic.

"The word of King Uffa himself. As I stood shivering in the darkness, keeping look-out as Sherlock Holmes had commanded me, a cold, iron hand suddenly took hold of my arm, and I turned around to find myself face-to-face with the ghost of the Saxon king, wild-eyed and haggard as he had appeared toward the end of his life. His rage-filled eyes staring out of the face-guard of his helmet gave the impression of a demonic mask.

"He spoke the language of his own time, of course, but fortunately I am sufficiently knowledgeable of Old English to have gotten the gist of what he said.

"He didn't care about the treasure, since gold is of no use to those who have passed beyond mortality. He wasn't even upset about his doom anymore, because he was with his beloved queen in some shadowy underworld known only to the heathen imagination of the Dark Age.

"But what did bother him was the infernal racket of hissing and growling and the gnashing of teeth, in short, the dragon. It still haunted his mound, devouring trespassers so noisily that the king and his wife could have no peace. He only wanted to be rid of it. He started to explain how the witch had carved the dragon's image onto an ivory plaque and placed it inside the mound. If that plaque were broken, the dragon would cease.

"'You mean there really *is* a dragon?' I asked him, in growing dread.

"He merely pointed. I turned. There, rising out of the fen, dripping faintly luminescent slime, hissing cold smoke, its eyes like dull red stars, was that very dragon which had devoured the king's thanes and Queen Hrothwealda, and had doubtless killed Ponderby too. It lurched toward me, its ragged, flightless wings rippling like tent flaps. Its voice was the roaring of a hurricane.

"The king offered me his sword and shield, but they were rusted and I could see they were no good. First I hurled one of the probing rods, and the monster reared up, howling, the rod sticking in its face like a pin. Then I fought it with my walking stick, and gave a good account of myself too, whacking it on the nose over and over, the way a trainer does with an unruly bear. I knew that Holmes, Watson, and Grice Paterson were in terrible danger, and the only hope was to lure the dragon away into the quicksand, where hopefully it would founder before I did.

"So I whacked it on the nose some more, shouted, and shone my torch into its eyes. I ran down the side of Uffa's mound, to where I expected to find a path. But somehow I had made a mistake in the dark. Almost at once I stumbled into the quicksand, losing both stick and torch. I clung to a bush, and could have extracted myself without much difficulty in a few minutes, but the dragon was upon me and I knew it was all up.

"Then, suddenly, as if by a miracle, and far more thoroughly than had ever Mrs. Grice Paterson, the dragon *vanished into thin air.*"

* * * * * * *

"How very convenient," said the Skeptic. "A miracle."

"So it seemed, but Holmes tells us that things are not what they merely seem. There really was a plaque of ivory, about four inches square, rudely carved with the figure of a dragon. It's in the British Museum now."

"I've never seen it there."

"It's not on public display because its condition, but it is there, in a drawer, broken in half, still marked with the inadvertent boot-print of the world's first and greatest consulting detective. The curator is an old friend. He showed it to me once."

The Skeptic was left thwarted, outflanked, and sputtering. The rest of us looked on with, I think, a certain satisfaction. But the Clubman's implacable foe grasped at one last, desperate straw.

"I demand to know," said he, "what *you* were doing on the fen that night. It was a rather large coincidence, you must admit. What *was* your urgent business, which you seem to have forgotten about afterward?"

The Clubman drank, and paused. There was a flicker of venomous triumph in the Skeptic's eyes.

The Clubman put down his glass. "I was looking for the Salmon of Knowledge. From the most ancient times, Britons have believed in an ageless fish which is the source of all wisdom and the guardian of whatever folk holds this island. When St. Augustine of Canterbury came to evangelize the heathen Saxons, he knew he had to convert the *fish* first, if he was to make any headway. In his *Life* there are certain clues, from which I deduced where he found it."

"Not in any version *I've* read—"

We ignored the Skeptic. The Clubman calmly continued. "I was there on that night because, like Grice Paterson, I was so excited by my discovery that I couldn't allow anyone else to beat me to it. The Salmon was there, too. I got to within ten yards of the pool in which it resided. But I was caught in the quicksand by then, and the dragon was upon me. The dragon saw the fish, and paused for just a second, long enough for Holmes to unwittingly save my life. The dragon swallowed the fish in one gulp, as an appetizer before the main course which was to be myself. Then, of course, the dragon vanished. But the fish was gone and it was too late. I think you will admit that the probity of the English race has declined somewhat since its loss."

He indicated the Boorish Member, still snoring, and not even the Skeptic could contradict him.

He held up his glass. "Waiter! Another whiskey!"

THE ADVENTURE OF THE HANOVERIAN VAMPIRES
(An Alternate Historical Vampire Cat Detective Story)

I found it. It was mine, a pretty, shiny thing, which I found amusing to swat about on the ground for several minutes, watching the evening sunlight gleam off the polished surface. Then, of course, I lost interest and left it where it lay. But it was still mine. So when one of the "street arabs"—verminous *boys*—snatched it up, I yowled in protest and gave the villain a fine raking on the calf.

He yowled right back and kicked me away. I landed nimbly and hissed, ready for another round of combat.

"What have you got there, Billy?" came another voice.

"I dunno, Mr. 'olmes."

"I'll give you a shilling for it."

The transaction was done, though the shiny object was still mine.

But now I was content, for the trouser leg I rubbed against belonged to the most perceptive of all human beings, the Great Detective himself, and the result of that encounter is the only Sherlock Holmes adventure ever narrated by a cat.

It is not possible for me to give you my name, for the true names of cats are never revealed outside our secretive tribe, and not even Sherlock Holmes may deduce them; whether the street arabs or Dr. Watson called me Fluffy or Mouser or something far less complimentary is, frankly, beneath notice. Suffice it to say that Holmes and I had a certain understanding by which we recognized and respected one another. You won't read of any of this in the chronicles penned by the doltish Watson, an altogether inferior lump of clay, *who once owned a bulldog pup,* probably without appreciating the crucial distinction that one *owns* a dog but *entertains* a cat. A dog is a useful object, even as, I suppose, Watson at times was useful.

But he tried to shoo me way, hissing, "Scat!" and other ridiculous imprecations, before Holmes drew his attention to the object in hand.

"It is the clue we have been seeking," said he. "Come Watson, we have much to do this night. It would be well if you brought your revolver."

Moments later, all three of us were clattering along the rapidly darkening streets of London in a Hansom. At first the driver, like the boorish Watson, objected to my presence, but Holmes gave the driver and extra coin. Watson, dog-like, acquiesced. Holmes would have found it useless to explain to him that cats partake of the most ancient mysteries of the dark, and so have a proper place in any night of intrigue and adventure.

It was indeed such a night.

As we wove through the narrow, filthy streets of the East End, past increasingly disreputable denizens, Holmes held up the shiny thing—which I now conceded I had *loaned* to Mr. Holmes.

"Deduce, Watson."

I assume this was a game for Holmes, like swatting a ball of string.

"It is a very thin locket," said Watson, "for I see that a spring-lock opens it—"

"Look out, Watson!" cried Holmes, for Watson had unthinkingly sprung open the locket, allowing a scrap of paper to flutter out. Deftly, Holmes snatched the paper out of the air.

"What is it, Holmes?"

"Momentarily, Watson. First, the locket."

"It and its chain are gold-plated."

"Not silver, Watson. Perhaps you will see the significance of that."

Obviously not. Watson continued. "On one side, is a female portrait—not an attractive one, I dare say—"

"I shall entirely trust your judgment in that department, Watson. Pray, continue."

"She wears a royal crown. The inscription is in German, and it reads: VICTORIA KAISERIN GROSS BRITANNIEN—Good God, Holmes!"

"Yes, Watson, it is the emblem of the current Hanoverian pretender, whose plottings against our king and country never cease, even after the failure—so ably chronicled by another writer—of the desperate scheme to place St. Paul's Cathedral on rollers and wheel it into the Thames, back in the days of James the Fourth."

"God save His Majesty, King James the Sixth, and all the House of Stuart!"

"A sentiment I echo, Watson, but we must hurry on and save the patriotism for our leisure. As you see, we are running out of time."

I placed my paws on the high dashboard of the Hansom for a better view. We were near the London docks. A fog had settled in among the poorly-lit streets. The air was thick with strange smells. Many of the passers-by were foreigners of the most unsavory sort.

"Recall, Watson," said Holmes, "that the notorious Dr. Moriarty, before he turned to crime, wrote, in addition to a curious monograph about an asteroid, a treatise on the possibility of an infinity of alternative worlds existing side by side, which may perhaps be *realized* by the use of certain potent objects—he actually used the word "numinous"—which suggest all manner of fantastic combinations, such as, for example, one in which Bonnie Prince Charlie was *defeated* at Culloden and England today is ruled by this same unhandsome *Victoria* of the House of Hanover—"

"Good God, Holmes!"

"You could as well imagine a world in which you, Watson, are Grand Panjandrum of Nabobistan, complete with harem. You would enjoy that, would you not?"

"I wouldn't be with you, Holmes," he said with some regret.

For an instant I almost admired Watson, though I knew his was mere dog-like loyalty.

"But to conclude," said Holmes, "it was Moriarty's theory, which I believe he has passed on to his Hanoverian confederates and which will perhaps be put to the test tonight, that with the use of such an object, *which has been manufactured in one of the alternative worlds and conjured into ours,* all manner of what the ignorant would call supernatural beings or creatures may be imposed—"

At that moment the Hansom came to a halt. We three debarked. The cab hurried off. I ran ahead of the two humans, into the gloom. The hideous smell of the river and of river rats was ahead of me.

Holmes and Watson hurried to keep pace with me, their great, clumsy feet thundering on the pavement. Dr. Watson gasped between breaths.

"This theory, Holmes, seems perfectly insane—"

"Watson, at such times it pays to be a little mad!"

"And you, the rationalist!"

Holmes made no reply to Watson's taunt, for we had come to our destination, a deserted wharf amid tumbledown warehouses. The fog was so thick it seemed a solid thing. Even I shivered.

Holmes struck a match for light. He held the paper from inside the locket up so Watson could read it.

"It is a shipping document," said Watson. "In receipt of five boxes of earth...what would anybody want with those, Holmes?"

"Observe the crest, Watson."

"An odd one. With a bat—"

"It is the arms of a certain *voivode* of Transylvania, a Count Dracula, about whom many terrible things are whispered. Now all the pieces of the puzzle come together. This Dracula, in the employ of the Hanoverians, under the direction of Moriarty—"

"I don't understand, Holmes."

Impatiently, Holmes got out the locket and showed Watson the reverse.

"It's the same crest, Holmes, to be sure, but—"

I let out a screech of challenge, and at this point Holmes had no time to deal with Watson's thick-headedness. A low, flat barge drifted out of the fog toward the wharf, heavily laden with long, rectangular boxes.

"Quick, Watson! Under no circumstances must that vessel be allowed to touch land!"

The two of them ran to the end of the wharf, and with a long leap all three of us landed squarely in the middle of the approaching barge. Watson's thick head proved to be of some service at this point, I must admit, because even as we landed one of those disreputable foreigners arose from behind one of the boxes and clubbed Watson with a stout cudgel, which would have broken his skull had it not been so thick, but instead sent him tumbling back against his assailant, who was thus set off balance.

Sherlock Holmes, strikingly agile for a human, had all the advantage he needed. He dealt with the single *live* crewman on the barge, leaving him unconscious at his feet.

But even he could not quite grasp the *true* danger. I was the one who first appreciated the significance of the horrible carrion smell which wafted from the boxes, now all the more intense as the lids of those boxes creaked and rose up, *opened from within*.

In the struggle, Holmes dropped the gold locket. It gleamed even in the poor light.

The *thing* which streaked out of one of the boxes far more swiftly than the other occupant could emerge went straight for the locket, swatted it to one side, then to the other, then turned to confront me.

"*Mine!*" I communicated, in the secret language of cats, which no human may ever understand.

When I call it a cat, I use the term loosely, for though it had the form of a huge, black-furred tom, it was a *dead* thing with burning red eyes and glistening fangs. We struggled even as Holmes and his opponents did, both seeking to regain the shiny locket-and-chain, while we rolled right to the edge of the barge's deck, mere inches above the noxious water.

That was when the inspiration came to me, though I paid a terrible price.

I let go of what was *mine*. Instantly my enemy grabbed hold of the chain with both forepaws and became entangled, and it took but a single swipe for me to knock him over the side into the water. The carrion-thing let out a hideous yowl, then *exploded* into steam upon contact with the water and was gone.

As was my pretty treasure.

* * * * * * *

The rest is less interesting. Holmes, seeing a variety of carrion *humans* emerging from the wooden boxes, heaved first the barge's anchor, then the semi-conscious Watson and the inert crewman over the side and leapt into the water himself. He stood up, awash to his shoulders. I might have been in a difficult situation had he not allowed me to ride atop his head all the way to shore, while he dragged Watson and the nautical thug.

Once on land, we watched the hideous spectacle of the carrion things stumbling about, seemingly unable to figure any way out of their present predicament.

"The vampires are rendered helpless by the running water of the good Thames," Holmes explained. "So enfeebled, they cannot even raise the anchor. Daylight will force them back into their boxes, where they are easily destroyed."

"What I don't understand," said Watson, the following morning, back in Baker Street, "is how the locket got there in the first place."

While they spoke, I lapped a well-deserved saucer of milk, despite Watson's disapproval.

"I think Count Dracula—who was not among the vampires destroyed, and has yet escaped us—was betrayed by his cat."

Holmes got out *the locket* and dangled it by its chain.

Watson stuttered. Even I looked up in amazement.

Holmes laughed. "When the sun rose and the tide went out, I hired one of the Irregulars to splash around in the shallow water until he found it."

The thought of a "street arab" immersing himself in the nasty element to recover my prize made me think that even boys have their uses.

"Dracula's feline," said Holmes, "must have passed from ship to shore many times, perhaps carried by a human agent, to serve as a scout. On one of those missions, it stole the crucial locket, then, losing interest, abandoned it. The object is a perfect cat-toy, don't you think?"

He dangled the beautiful thing on its chain. I watched, fascinated. But I continued with my milk. It was *mine,* after all, and I could play with it later.

ABOUT THE AUTHOR

ROBERT REGINALD was born in Japan, and lived in Turkey as a youth. He starting writing as a child, and penned his first book during his senior year in college. He settled in Southern California in 1969, where he served as an academic librarian for forty years. He currently edits the Borgo Press Imprint of Wildside Press, and has also penned more than 100 books and 13,000 short pieces.

His recent works of fiction include: four Nova Europa historical fantasies, *The Dark-Haired Man; or, The Hieromonk's Tale* (2004), *The Exiled Prince; or, The Archquisitor's Tale* (2004), *Quæstiones; or, The Protopresbyter's Tale* (2005), and *The Fourth Elephant's Egg; or, The Hypatomancer's Tale* (forthcoming); four science fiction novels, *Invasion!: Earth vs. the Aliens* (2007; a trilogy comprising *War of Two Worlds*, *Operation: Crimson Storm*, and *The Martians Strike Back!*), *Knack' Attack: A Tale of the Human-Knacker War* (2010), *"A Glorious Death": A Tale of the Human-Knacker War* (forthcoming), and *Academentia: A Future Dystopia* (forthcoming); two Phantom Detective period mysteries, *The Phantom's Phantom* (2007) and *The Nasty Gnomes* (2008); a comic mystery, *The Paperback Show Murders* (forthcoming); and three story collections, *Katydid & Other Critters: Tales of Fantasy and Mystery* (2001), *The Elder of Days: Tales of the Elders* (2010), and *The Judgment of the Gods and Other Verdicts of History* (2011).

He loves to hear from his readers. You can find him at:
www.millefleurs.tv

ABOUT THE AUTHOR

DARRELL SCHWEITZER is a four-time World Fantasy Award finalist, and one-time winner, and the author of *The Mask of the Sorceror*, *The White Isle*, *The Shattered Goddess*, *We Are All Legends*, *Living with the Dead*, and much more. His nearly three hundred short stories have appeared in *Alfred Hitchcock's Mystery Magazine*, *Cemetery Dance*, *Twilight Zone*, *Night Cry*, *Whispers*, *Interzone*, *Amazing Stories*, and in numerous anthologies. He co-edited *Weird Tales* magazine for nineteen years, and has also edited several anthologies, including (with Martin H. Greenberg) *The Secret History of Vampires*, *Cthulhu's Reign*, and *Full Moon City*. With George H. Scithers, he edited *Tales from the Spaceport Bar* and *Another Round at the Spaceport Bar*. He has written several books about H. P. Lovecraft and Lord Dunsany. He is also a well-known interviewer, poet, reviewer, and essayist, whose work has appeared in *The Washington Post*, *Publishers Weekly*, *Foundation*, and *The New York Review of Science Fiction*.

THE VERDICT OF HISTORY

Here are four scintillating tales of detection set in ancient and medieval times:

In "The Judgment of the Gods," a young Greek trader is challenged by the Assyrian King-to-be, Esarhaddon, to uncover the murderer of his father, King Sennacherib. In "Occam's Razor," evil Pope John XXII forces the great medieval philosopher, Father William of Occam, to investigate the deaths of French King Philip IV and Pope Clement V, both of whom were involved in the suppression of the Templar Order.

In "Occam's Treasure," William must uncover the mysterious fiend who is killing high-ranking churchmen in Avignon, and leaving a silver coin on their tongues as his calling card. Occam then faces his greatest challenge in "Occam's Measure," trying to stop a vicious serial murderer haunting the night-time alleyways of the Papal city.

Great mystery—and fantasy—reading!

Selected Borgo Press Books by ROBERT REGINALD

Academentia: A Future Dystopia
Ancestral Voices: An Anthology of Early Science Fiction
Ancient Hauntings (ed. with Douglas Menville)
The Attempted Assassination of John F. Kennedy
BP 300: A Bibliography of the Borgo Press, 1976-1998
Choice Words: Writers Writing About Writing (editor)
Classics of Fantastic Literature (with Douglas Menville)
Codex Derynianus III (with Katherine Kurtz)
The Dark-Haired Man; or, The Hieromonk's Tale (NE #1)
Dreamers of Dreams (ed. with Douglas Menville)
The Exiled Prince; or, The Archquisitor's Tale (NE #2)
Forgotten Fantasy: Issues #1-5 (ed. with Douglas Menville)
The Fourth Elephant's Egg; or, The Hypatomancer's Tale (#4)
"A Glorious Death": The Human-Knacker War, Book Three
The House of the Burgesses (with Mary A. Burgess)
If J.F.K. Had Lived (with Jeffrey M. Elliot)
The Judgment of the Gods and Other Verdicts of History
King Solomon's Children (ed. with Douglas Menville)
Knack' Attack: A Tale of the Human-Knacker War (Book Two)
The Martians Strike Back!: Invasion! Earth vs. the Aliens (#3)
The Nasty Gnomes: A Novel of the Phantom Detective—#2
Operation Crimson Storm: Invasion! Earth vs. the Aliens (#2)
The Paperback Show Murders
Phantasmagoria (ed. with Douglas Menville)
The Phantom's Phantom: A Novel of the Phantom Detective—#1
Quæstiones; or, The Protopresbyter's Tale (Nova Europa #3)
R.I.P. (ed. with Douglas Menville)
The Spectre Bridegroom and Other Horrors (ed. with Menville)
They (ed. with Douglas Menville)
Trilobite Dreams; or, The Autodidact's Tale: An Autobiography
War of Two Worlds: Invasion! Earth vs. the Aliens (#1)
Worlds of Never (ed. with Douglas Menville)
Xenograffiti: Essays on Fantastic Literature